To Love Again

To Love Again

Carroll Rinehart

Rinehart Books   Tucson, Arizona

This edition was prepared for publishing by
Ghost River Images
5350 East Fourth Street
Tucson, Arizona 85711
www.ghostriverimages.com

ISBN 978-0-9898222-0-6

Library of Congress Control Number: 2013914433

Printed in the United States of America

August, 2013

10 9 8 7 6 5 4 3 2 1

Contents

End of Summer

The end of summer in Baronsville, Ohio, is a time of waiting. The time in the 1950s is like each year. Much like an old man sitting on his rocker on the front porch of his farm, there is the remembering of the days gone by.

The tulips, daffodils and crocus which peeped out in early spring, then displayed their glory in their color and green wraps, have passed on with only the faded reminder of where they once stood.

All the summer flowers seem to cry out for water with an unquenchable thirst that cannot be met with dew or rain alone. They stand tired and waiting, leaves drooping, pods of seeds forming to complete what nature has intended them to do. Now goldenrod dominates the roadside and the nostrils of the villagers, invoking sneezes and wheezes.

Fields of grain, once green with spring's promise, followed by their ripening seasons, waving and dancing in sequence across their stage to the gentle music of a morning breeze, are gone. Now, harvested, only the golden stubble remains as a reminder of their once glorious presence. Now those spiked stubble remains pounded into the fields to hold the soil in place while awaiting the preparation for a new crop.

Fields of corn needed to be knee high by the Fourth of July. Once, in the earliest days of youth, the corn produced lunch for the hungry; now, in shocks, they stand bound together like teepees in an Indian village. Only now they await the time when they will be unmasked and the fruits of their being are extracted for the use for which they were given life.

The beginning of school marks the end of summer. Children await the sound of the school bell. Some are eager to explore new worlds - others resist, wanting to continue freedom from study, to be able to explore their worlds through play.

Teachers await their students. How will they engage them? What challenges await? How can one keep those skills that must be taught, fresh and with imagination?

August and September are times of waiting, times to remember what has been, and to be curious for what tomorrow may bring.

Chapter 1

Monday Morning

One can always tell it's Monday and the time is 6:00 am. The farmers and men of the village of Baronsville enter Alice's Diner. The game of who can mount their hats on the hall tree is the first agenda of their playful business. As they enter, there is the graceful, and sometimes ungraceful, moment of sailing hats to the top of their perch. Those that miss are required to retrieve their hats and slump in disgrace to their place at the table.

"I seen they parked a lot of heavy equipment in the fields of Sam Dawson's farm over the weekend," Sam Brewer said, starting the conversation.

"I guess the guy from Bloomfield who bought the place wants to build houses on it."

"I hear'd he's buildin' some purty fancy places on one acre lots."

"How many acres on Sam's old place?"

"If'n I remember right, it's one hundred and sixty acres in the farm."

"Someone tole me he paid a right big price for the place. 'Spect to make it all back with people wantin' to get out of the big city of Bloomfield." Sam continued.

"Someone tole me a guy wanted to buy the barn that's across

the road from Sam's house. Wants to make a big restaurant in it."

"A big restaurant in Baronsville? The guy' must be outa his mind."

"Speakin' of restaurants, maybe we otta order. Lily kain't wait forever to cook fer us hungry clods."

"Alice, you servin' grub to a bunch of no-counts?"

Watching from her place by the cash register, Alice smiled at the way these grown men played together. Always the same. Always fun. Grabbing her order pad, she made her way to their table.

"Okay, you outlaws, what'll it be today? The usual?

Billy Burch was the first to order. "Gotta change my order. The little woman read in her woman's mag that too much fried food ain't good fer the system. Better make my eggs poached. When I tell her what I did, I might even make some points. I need all the help I can git!"

"Poached it will be. What'da ya want with it? Potatoes or somethin' else?" Alice asked.

"Kan't reform all at once. Fried potatoes. I won't hav'ta confess that. And some of Lily's home-made bread, toasted, should make a workin' man's body in good shape to start the day."

One by one they ordered, most all ordering the same thing they ordered every Monday morning.

"Thanks, guys, what would Monday be without all your nonsense? Anyway, how could a working girl keep up on all the community gossip without your help?" With her orders in hand, Alice moved to the window, giving the orders to Lily, who smiled at the playfulness of grown men.

"Okay, guys, back to the important business of the day. Who was the guy that bought Sam's farm?"

"His last name is Roberts, I think, 'tho few of us ever got acquainted with the guy. Someone said he seen him at the Sohio station getting gas one mornin'. Said he got his gas, paid the man, and jumped into his car, sayin', "Gotta get goin', I'm late for my golf.""

"At least we know what was important for a guy on the run!"

"I hear'd he was applyin' for the prez positions at Supreme

Foods, but didn't get it."

"Rumor has it he drunk himself silly until he really passed out."

"My kids tol' me he never got home to see his son off to the air force fer trainin."

"Ain't that the kid who got the O'Conner girl pregnant?"

"And got himself killed drivin' too fast on a weekend pass?"

"I hear'd he'd been drinkin' with his air force buddy. They took the one girl's sports car' n went fer a drive. With the two guys and two girls, you know what was on their minds!"

"Doubt it was plannin' to go to a Sunday School picnic!"

"Accordin' to the Bloomfield News, they crashed, killin' the two guys and one girl. One survived. I hear'd she's bound to a wheelchair fer the resta her life."

"We did get to know Mrs. Roberts. She came to church 'most every Sunday, a good woman."

"The Roberts, they were purty hush-hush about their separation and divorce."

"Divorce is purty rare in Baronsville."

Marriage is fer better or worse. I wished there was more of those better times. Couldn't be a problem on my part."

"Taint what my misses tells me, Barry. Your better half, I hear is the better!"

"So what happened to this Roberts guy? Has anyone seen him?"

"I hear'd he moved back to Bloomfield. Nobody's seen hide nor hair of him since!"

The last morsel, now history, brings the gathering to an end. Retrieving their hats, paying their bills, and depositing tips on the table, and having shared the important news of the day, each of the men left to go to work.

Chapter 2

In a One Room Apartment

Following the sale of the farm in Baronsville, Ohio, Martin Mitchell Roberts rented a cheap, one room apartment across from a park in Bloomfield. And because everyone from his former life knew him as Mitch, he began using his first name in a sobering admission that he was no longer the person he had been.

The apartment was a place to get lost.

In one corner there was a stove, a refrigerator, a sink, and a can for trash. The refrigerator was almost empty of food. It had little more than an opened package of hot dogs, a can of mustard, and a bottle of milk. Above the sink was a shelf, dominated by one box of cereal. A couple of plates and a bowl shared the shelf,

A small table and two chairs were near the center of the room. Dirty plates, glasses, forks, and spoons were often left in place.

A small room had been carved out of the cramped space to house a toilet, wash bowl and shower. It was so small, one had to step outside in the room to change his mind.

A bed found its place against the far wall. The few covers needed in the late summer heat were left crumpled in a pile exactly where they had been thrown back when the sleeper answered his rushed morning call to the bathroom.

Martin's golf bag and clubs leaned against an empty, uncommitted corner of the room. Since moving into the room, they had not left the spot where they had been thrust. Oh yes, there was one time that they were packed in the car, and taken to the Bloomfield Country Club.

Even with his appearance of carelessness, a heavy beard, unkempt clothes, and disheveled hair, a young club staff person recognized him. "Gonna play a round, Mitch? Meetin' someone this mornin'?"

"Not meetin' anybody. I was hopin' I could join some others."

"Tain't the Mitch Roberts I useta know. Ain't never seen you play without somebody that was really somebody."

He found another couple that allowed him to join them. They had nothing in common. Conversations were almost impossible to get started. He felt like an outsider, alone, even when he was with them. Their talk was about their family, and the tasks to be done following the game. When they arrived at the seventh hole, the game was so void of enjoyment that he excused himself, picked up his bag, and retreated to his car for the quiet drive back to his apartment. The bag and the clubs were put back in their place, and not invited out again.

The nights were some of the loneliest times. Following "dinner," a hot dog, or a hamburger from a fast food place, Martin would sit alone awaiting time to go to bed. No pictures were on the wall to soften the space. He seldom turned the small television set on to help pass the time. When the light from the single bulb in the center of the ceiling was turned off, there was only the dim intrusion of the street lights to soften the space. Being on the second floor, he sometime never even drew the shade. Even when the shades were drawn, a split in the shade entertained a streak of light that framed itself on the wall near his bed.

Nights seemed to never end. Time after time, Martin would remain awake, looking upward to the ceiling. There were times when the ceiling became a screen, where, in his imagination and his memory, he would see the events that brought him to this place. The pictures in his mind were painful. He tried to make them go away, but they would not do as he wanted. A good night's sleep was difficult to attain.

At times he could not stand the room longer. Following a bowl of cereal, some milk, and a cup of coffee, leaving everything in place, he would try to escape from his memories. He would go to the park across the street. There he sat looking off into space. No sense of the space and the things about him entertained his thoughts. It was as if time and life stood still.

Chapter 3

Escaping To The Park

Beatrice Bonner would arise each morning, ease herself into her wheelchair, and engage the bathroom facilities, before making her breakfast. Once all that was history, she would return to her room and strap her braces to her legs, before wheeling to the apartment parking garage for her car.

She would drive to her office on the far side of the park, the area opposite Martin's one room apartment. Parking the car, she would retrieve her wheelchair and take herself across the street to the park. She loved the fresh smell of the newly watered grass, flowers, and shrubs, something that didn't make it with the planter box in the window of her apartment. Often she would be delighted when mothers would bring their young children to play on the equipment. What greater music than the sound of joyous screams, rushing down a slide, or hanging on tightly, while a mother turned the merry-go-round! Joy and life was everywhere!

One day she looked at a man sitting alone on a bench. His face showed no feeling, no smiles to show interest in the space he filled. His eyes were looking forward, but seemingly not seeing anything. What was he seeing? Was it an imaginary screen upon which stories were being told? What was being retold in his memory? Why, at times, did he close his eyes and tighten the muscles in his face, as though he was in pain?

Could he enjoy the flowers and the smell of the freshly watered plants? What could he be seeing? He never turned his head to take in the things happening in the park. His face hosted a heavy beard. His hair appeared to be "combed" by running his fingers through it. The mustard spot on his shirt spoke of a previous meal. Mustard could not hide the fine quality of his shirt. Nor could the wrinkles in his pants deny their richness. What happened to this man to cause such a state of carelessness?

Each day, on her way back to the office, she would wheel by him with a good morning greeting. At first there was absolutely no response. After several days the man nodded his head in response. There was a day when she greeted him with a, "Good morning," and he echoed, "Good morning."

It was on Wednesday of the third week that Beatrice Bonner wheeled herself, in her escape to the park, that the miracle of miracles happened. Clouds blocked the sun. The air felt heavy with moisture. For some reason she had the urge to go to the park. There was a heaviness, but joy was present in the space. Even though mothers didn't bring their children to play, Beatrice could almost hear, in her imagination, their screams of delight.

The same man had come to the park to escape the loneliness of his room. He sat silently as he had done day after day. He little noticed Beatrice Bonner's presence in the park. For some reason he felt alone in the world. A part of him wanted to cry out for help, but he didn't know how to ask for it. His life had always been one of fierce independence, of going it alone.

Suddenly Beatrice felt a rain drop. "I must hurry to my office or I'll get drenched." The raindrops began to increase. She began her rush to her office. As she came to the lonely man, she said, "Sir, would you please help me get across the street to my office?"

The man jumped up, got behind the wheelchair, and began rushing across the street to the handicap entrance to the building. They had just gotten inside when the rainclouds dropped their load - torrents of rain came down in sheets.

Once inside, Martin looked at the lady for the first time. He saw raindrops, like dew on the grass, giving life and presence to her face, or was it tears of joy sent from heaven? Then she lifted her hands with fingers that could caress anything they touched, and she brushed the raindrops from her face, revealing a soft sensuous skin. "Wow! We made it just in time. Thank you, friend," she added.

Through the torrents came a woman shielded by an umbrella. "Good morning, Doctor Bonner. Do you think it will rain?"

"I'm sure it will. Betsy Blair, this man got me from the park, just in time. Betsy this is - good grief, I don't know your name."

"It's Martin Roberts. Not much more to tell," Martin said, not wanting to tell more.

`"I guess I should introduce myself. I'm Beatrice Bonner."

"It looks and sounds like we're in for a big one!" Betsy volunteered. "I best get to my office and get started on my work."

Beatrice followed, "Martin, why don't you come to my office until the rain stops?"

"Oh I couldn't. I'm a mess. I feel like a bum. I'm not dressed to be in a place like this."

"Never have found anything in any writings that says you have to appear in any set way to be in a church. Push me on to my office. I'm sure that someone has had the coffee pot going and there are usually some good yummies to soak up the coffee."

Reluctantly, Martin pushed her to her office. He glanced at the book titles on the shelves. Not since his days at Ohio State had he been reminded of authors he was invited to read, authors that opened him up to the world.

His eyes were drawn to Beatrice. Her soft, golden blond hair, outlining her face and reaching downward in soft curls, graced her shoulders. Her eyes, seemingly all knowing, followed the every movement of his eyes and, in turn, smiled with sensitivity and seductiveness. His eyes viewed every part of her body, supplying his own image when it was not available while she sat in her wheelchair. His eyes rested on her legs.

Martin saw the braces on Beatrice's legs. Beatrice was aware

17

he was looking at her braces.

"I'll bet you're wondering what caused me to need braces on my legs?" He nodded his concern. Beatrice continued, "When I was seven years old, I came down with polio. I am told that I almost died. I was loved back to life. Now every cell in my body knows the meaning of love. The gift of that experience is that I am called to invite others to life through the power of love. I also know that I have a body, but I am more than my body!"

"Wow! Roberto Assagioli stuff!" Martin replied.

"So, how do you know about Roberto Assagioli?" she asked.

"Something I remember form a psychology class I had at Ohio State."

"Man, that's heavy stuff. I'm impressed. We must talk more about that."

The conversation continued with bits of information from their histories being shared. As they continued to talk, Martin became aware of the time which had passed. "Look the sun is shining. It's time I leave you to your work. Thank you for sharing the time. Thanks to whatever brought the rain about. This has been the most time I've ever spent in a church in my whole life."

The comment brought a smile to Beatrice's face. "And thank you for bringing me in out of the rain. If people would have seen us, racing from the park, and heard the laughter while running, they would have thought we were a couple of young kids playing a new game."

Her words brought a smile to Martin's face. Not having anything with him, except the clothes on his back, he said his goodbyes and headed back to his apartment. Something had changed about him, and beginning to change within him. But where would it lead him?

When he looked at the room, it was as if it were for the very first time.

"What a dismal place. Four walls and some things scattered about." Talking to himself, he thought, "Man, you gotta get some things together." All began to go well, until he picked up the graduation picture of his son, Jack. Holding the picture in his hands he sank on the bed, wanting to cry, but tears would not come. Suddenly his grief overcame him. He replayed in his memory, the times he had been so intent on making things his own way, that he was never present to, or with, his son. He remembered the times, coming home from work, he would see Gladys, his wife, teaching their son how to catch and bat a ball. Suddenly his memory and imagination would bring into view the story of Jack's accident and his death. It was an overwhelming sadness. Nothing seemed to matter. "What a failure I've been!" There was the urge to escape his memories. But how does one escape memories? "Oh, God, help me!"

Solving life problems, such as this, were never taught at the University. The journey to wholeness is sometimes long and difficult, but it is a journey that has to be taken.

Martin wasn't sure how long he remained in his state of depression. He was only aware that the room had darkened. Only the street light broke the darkness. Drawing the shade, he glanced at the streak of light that found its way through the slit in the shade and announced itself on the wall above his bed. He removed his yellow-decorated, mustard-stained shirt, and threw it on the chair beside his bed. Removing his pants, he threw those across the chair, also. Now down to his undershorts, he slipped into bed. Closing his eyes, he attempted to go to sleep. Sleep would not come. Memories would not let go of him. "Go away! Go away. Let me be!" he seemed to say over and over in his mind, but they would not go.

Finally, utterly fatigued, he was able to release the memories. The hour was late. So much had happened in this one day. What was its meaning? What was its purpose? Why was the rain so refreshing? Why was it so different from other rains? And who is this Beatrice Bonner? Why did she happen to be in the park just before the rain storm? With so many questions racing through his mind, he was at last sound asleep.

Chapter 4

Then Came Thursday

Daylight had replaced the street lights, when Martin Roberts stretched his body under the sheet. The night was refreshing, even during the times when his memory replayed the events of yesterday. What was so special about yesterday? The daily routine began as most days: a bowl of cereal and then escaping from his room and going to the park. It began as always, sitting alone on a bench, looking but not seeing, seldom listening to the birds offering their morning songs, or being aware of the freshness of the newly-watered grass and plants.

A part of him seemed to say, "What have we been trying to achieve? Your whole life is not a waste of time. People will respect you if you really achieve, and you'll be important because of what you are able to do. Don't give up now just because you didn't get the president position of Supreme Foods. No one likes a quitter! Somebody wants what you have to give! Keep pushing, man!"

Another part of him remembered the rain storm. He thought, "Then it began to rain and a woman in a wheelchair invited me to push her to her office. Something began to change. What was it that presented itself as a gift? What was there in the pushing of a wheelchair to avoid a drenching by the rain that began some change in me? And why, when the woman said, 'I have braces, but I'm more than my braces,' did I reply, almost without thinking, 'Roberto Assagioli'? Why am I thinking so much about Assagioli?"

His memory was flooded often in the night with the memory of the beautiful girl's golden blond hair and the invitations he saw in her smile.

Martin threw the sheet covering his body aside. He took a moment to sense the coolness of the morning. Even the presence of his undershorts seemed too confining. He sprang into a sitting position at the side of the bed. Removing his shorts he headed for the shower, singing a song he had learned as a child. "Eency weency spider went up the water spout. Down came the rain and washed the spider out. Out came the sun and dried up all the rain. And the eency, weency spider went up the spout again."

The sound of the shower, like the rain, seemed to call forth the memories of yesterday. Following the shower, he applied shaving cream to his face, and with a razor in hand, removed his beard of several days. A sigh of disappointment accompanied the absence of after shave lotion. The comb made sure that every hair was in place. The tooth brush and mouth wash sweetened his breath.

A clean shirt and pressed pants completed the new ritual. Martin Roberts forgot breakfast as he rushed down the stairs and across the street to his bench in the park.

As he entered the park, he was fully aware of the watering of the grass and the plants. "How could I have missed all this at other times I came to the park? Listen to the birds as they share their morning songs!"

He smiled watching the squirrels playing about on the limbs of the trees spread above him.

Everything felt so alive.

His face would turn toward the pathway leading to the church. Excitedly he saw someone coming toward him. Was it the girl with the golden blond hair with her invitations? But it wasn't who he had wanted to see. It was only workmen coming to clean up the area following the storm. As they passed by him picking up broken branches, they greeted him warmly. "Good morning, sir. Quite a storm yesterday! It messed up a lot of stuff here in the park!"

Martin nodded his head and , "Uh huh!"

He continued to sit on his bench. A sense of loneliness came over him. He could no longer hear the birds singing. No mothers and their children came to play. Flowers had lost their appeal.

He again looked forward without seeing. Within his imagination and memory, he saw himself as a ten year old, and a fourth grader in school. Suddenly he could hear again the bullies of the class chanting, "Here comes smarty Marty, who wants to join our party. Come on guys, let's run and hide." They would run off, leaving him standing alone. As he remembered, his eye closed and the face muscles tightened, as if to shut out the pain. He wasn't sure how long he sat there. Time seemed to stand still.

When he finally realized where he was and that he had not eaten, he took himself to the a little "hole in the wall" restaurant. Martin ordered breakfast: two eggs-over easy, toast and grits. When they came, it was not appealing. "Eating alone is not much fun," he thought to himself. He ate at it, then pushed it aside. "What if she comes to the park while I'm here feeding my face?" he thought.

Paying his bill and leaving a tip, he rushed back to his bench in the park. No one was in sight. The sense of loneliness returned. The fourth grade bully chant kept ringing in his ears, "Here comes smarty Marty, who wants to join our party. Come on, guys, let's run and hide!"

Time passed ever more slowly. His sense of being a loser came loudly to his mind. "If I can't find what I want here, where can I hide?" At long last he decided to go back to his room. "There, no one will find me."

He looked one more time to the pathway leading to the street and the church. Seeing nothing, with shoulder sagging and head bowed, he rose to return to his room.

He had taken but a few step, when he heard a loud shout, "Martin, Martin, where are you going? Wait for me. Sorry not to have come to the park earlier."

Martin quickly turned around. A smile covered his face. "Are you expecting another cloudburst? What surprise do you have for this old loser today?"

"I got busy with things that had to be taken care of this morning. One was planning a breakfast for people in the neighborhood. Students from Lily Wong's Cooking School are going to prepare breakfast. It's one of their special breakfasts, omelets that you'd never believe, omelets that one would almost die for! I'd like you to join us Saturday morning. It would give you a chance to meet some of your neighbors."

"Oh, no!" he thought, "Who would want to meet a loser? This would really blow my cover. I'm trying to get away and she is trying to get me to meet more people. Can I trust myself? What if I get hurt again? Will that drive me more deeply into my feeling of no-self worth?"

"Well, are you available, or is your social calendar filled?"

Beatrice for a moment looked Martin over. "Where's that guy that pushed me between raindrops yesterday? He had a beard. I can't believe my eyes. Hey, you're one handsome dude!"

"Flattery will get what one wants every time. Oh, okay, I'll come. Did you say Saturday? What time?"

"The young people will begin serving at eight o'clock. You might like to come a bit earlier to meet some neighbors, and choose what you want in your omelet. It has to be on Saturday because the students, normally, are in school during the week days. It is early because the students must get back to the Cooking School to work with Mrs. Wong."

Martin thought, "Where have I heard of Lily Wong's Cooking School before?"

"I know there's no cloudburst, but pushing me back to my office would be a most wonderful gift," Beatrice continued. "We could talk more about Assagioli. I have been very impressed with his view of people and their growth. Interested?"

"Are people interested in an omelet for breakfast? Does water run down hill? Do Catholics want to know who their Pope is? How fast do you want to go? Is there a speed limit on your vehicle?"

Martin got up and taking the handles of the wheelchair, the two playfully raced to the entrance of the church.

"You know the route to my office. If traffic is heavy, I'll use hand signals to let others know where we're headed."

"What is there about this woman that invites such playfulness from an old loser?" Martin thought to himself. "How is it she can turn a stormy day into sunshine? How does she invite my eyes to see those things that are always before me, but which I often fail to see?"

Chapter 5

In Dr. Bonner's Study

Martin pushed the wheelchair to Beatrice's study. Once inside, she wheeled herself to a spot across from where Martin had seated himself. Neither of them spoke. They looked at each other, as if wondering how to begin the conversation. He saw her beauty and the purposefulness in everything she said and did.

Martin, by his own confession, admitted he had had almost no connection with the working of the church. Dr. Bonner was unsure just how he might respond, if she began to ask the wrong questions. Martin cleared his throat, and the silence was beginning to be uncomfortable. Beatrice, understanding their discomfort, smiled at the action.

She began, "Why am I so uncomfortable in beginning a conversation? Is it because I know so little about you? Or perhaps, I am afraid I might begin in the wrong way? What is there about you that I find most interesting? Is it about my discovering that you are informed about things that are in my field? What is it that goes on within your mind?"

Martin replied, "I was intrigued with your ability to be playful, to see joy in everything going on. Is that something that I am searching to find in my life? When you said, 'I have braces, but I am more than these braces,' that triggered within me a part of my own history. I was surprised at how naturally it happened and how freely my response came. I had not thought about Assagioli since my college class. Assagioli was a psychologist living in the time of Sigmumd Freud and Karl Jung. How can I feel trust and at a level I seldom feel"

Dr. Bonner continued, "Trust is a most important part in our lives. When I contacted polio as a child, I did not fully understand why that had to happen to me. There's a part of me that still asks that question, although as I become older, more truth is revealed to me. Perhaps even being saved from a cloudburst, may have a message for me. We are never sure of the message, until we can look back upon it. Often times we almost have to reach a terrible bottom before we can reach up, but learning to reach up is necessary. Psychologists sometimes tell us we lead, not out of our strengths, but out of our vulnerability, that process of becoming fully known."

"If I were to become fully known, is there the possibility that I might experience rejection, and be hurt more deeply? I know hurt. I know how to hide. I know what it feels like to be a loser," Martin confessed.

"To paraphrase Assagioli, he might say, 'I am a loser , but I am more than a loser.' Perhaps that is where one might begin," Dr. Bonner added.

"This is heavy stuff, much to think about. Now, how to get around the ideas that we're exploring," Martin said, trying to bring the discussion to a temporary halt.

"I sense that we've gone very far in a short time. Perhaps it is best that we give the thoughts time to work their way through our minds. Anyway, I will see you on Saturday at the breakfast. Don't forget the students serve at eight. Come a little before to meet others from the neighborhood and to make your choice for the omelet." She turned her chair around to begin her work at her desk. "Thank you for sharing. You made it easy to begin our conversation."

Martin moved over toward her, as if to make physical contact but stopped, not sure how to say his good-bye. To feel her skin and to lift away her blond hair filled his imagination. He smiled, nodded his head in appreciation, and quietly left her study.

"Man, that was quite a session," he thought as he made his way out of the building, across the street, and to his bench in the park. "A part of me wants to share my thoughts with her, but another part of me isn't sure it's safe. But then, what do I have to lose? Can I go any lower than I've been feeling?" Martin sat on the bench, looking forward, allowing his mind to begin thinking what the next time with her will bring. "It's amazing, what's going on in my head. Think! Think! Think!"

Chapter 6

Within His Private Space

Upon Martin's return to his one room apartment, he decided to take care of the space in which he was living. He decided he needed something to make the room feel softer and more personal. What did he have that could be hung on the walls to soften their harshness? Pictures! Pictures would make it feel like he belonged in the space. What did he have to frame and hang? He looked in a box of keepsakes that he kept for some reason- maybe a picture of Jack. He had the high school graduation picture. There was another of Jack with his mother, when she was coaching him in shooting basketballs. It was a picture taken at their home in Bloomfield when Jack was an elementary school student. Martin's wife, Gladys, had insisted on having a hoop and backboard. He didn't have time, so she hired a man to install it. Jack would practice for hours, improving his skill with the basketball.

Recalling the details of Gladys' work with Jack, and his being unavailable for him was depressing. He placed the picture back in the box before walking to the window to look out upon the park. "How can I ever let go of these memories?" he asked himself. "What do I have to do to begin anew? What was driving me to fail a son who was a most important part of my life? Why didn't I know how to express my caring? Why am I standing here, looking out upon the park? Is there hope for me to be found in that space? Am I expecting something from the girl in her wheelchair?"

He had not eaten since mid-morning when he went to his most often visited restaurant. But where could he go? There was the Athletic Club, but Judy would know him, and he didn't want to have a drink. The memories of his last time at the Athletic Club were very painful, his intoxication following his not getting the presidency of Supreme Food Products. His missing his son's leaving for service was a pain he didn't want to remember. No point in getting caught up in more of those bad memories. The counter at the Dairy Store will have sandwiches, salads, and some small offerings. There are always ice cream treats for dessert.

Martin made his way to the Ice Cream shop. He ordered a hamburger, French fries, and a chocolate malt shake to top it off. He was so hungry. It was so good, like having a wonderful steak dinner with all the trimmings. Being able to concentrate on the food and none of his memories was a refreshing time for him. Paying his bill and leaving the usual ten percent tip, he headed out of the store and back to his apartment. No more memories today. But how do I let go of them?

The radio on the stand by his bed had not been turned on since he moved into the room. Going over to the bed, he reached over to turn on the radio. He dialed WOSU, the classical music station from The Ohio State University. They were playing the Schubert "Unfinished Symphony". He had heard it so often that he found himself humming the melodies. Music is so relaxing, a powerful way to escape.

After listening to several other compositions, he became aware that the room had darkened and the only light was from the street light, just outside his window. He turned down the sheet, undressed, laying his clothes carefully on the chair. Crawling into bed, he quickly dozed off to the Brahms Symphony No. 4. What a way to go!

Chapter 7

Friday - Alone

"Oh, no! Not now! Let me be. I want to sleep," Martin uttered half asleep. "Go away. You've interrupted my sleep all night!"

He stretched himself out and drew the sheet about him as if to shed the cold from his body. The covers on his bed displayed the struggles of the night. All night long he had tossed about in his bed until now his head and his pillow had taken up residence at the foot of the bed.

He tried to go back to sleep but his thoughts would not allow it.

"Go away! Stop bothering me! What do you want from me? Let me rest. I wanna be alone. No, that's not true. Where's Dr. Bonner when I need her?"

So began the first moments of Friday.

The days were becoming shorter. There was a sliver of light from the street light outside his room. The light, which pierced through the slit in the shade, stayed motionless on the wall beside him and on the ceiling above him. A stillness punctuated the room, as if all of life was suspended. It was as if all life awaited the right to move on.

Martin pinched his body as if to check on his own aliveness. He looked about himself and listened. Was the room and the stillness trying to tell him something?

"I will not leave this place until I can hear what is being said to me," he thought to himself. "Tell me what I'm supposed to hear!" No voices spoke. Nothing moved. All was stillness.

He cautiously threw back the sheet awaiting a reply. Nothing came. "I won't leave you, whoever you are, until you tell me what you want me to hear. I don't care how long it will take."

"Room with almost nothing in it, what may I hear from you? Your walls need paint. Nothing is hung to soften the space. Why? What do you want from me? Why did I choose you for a place to be?

Light bulb, shed more light. Can you show me what I am to know? How long must I wait? When will someone tell me what I need to know?"

He turned on the single light bulb hanging from the center of the ceiling. He turned on the one above the sink in the bathroom. And then he turned on the light above the stove and sink area. He rushed over to allow the shade at the window to be raised. "Light! Light! Help me know what I'm to know. Let me see." Nothing came.

Martin sank into a chair at the small table. "I must get myself something to eat." He lifted the nearly empty box of cereal from the shelf above the sink. He poured the contents into a bowl. "Nearly empty! Is this what I'm to know? Am I to know the emptiness in my life? What causes emptiness? The outer shell of the box didn't change, only the contents within!" He poured the milk over the cereal, then taking a bite explained, "Sour! The milk is sour! How long has it been in the 'fridge?' Milk, milk, what are you telling me?

It was as if everything in the room was breaking in upon his consciousness. "Let me out of this place. I'm not prepared to hear what you're trying to say to me. I'll find peace in the park."

Martin flushed his cereal down the toilet. "There! Gone are my problems. Gone! Away with whatever you might have said to me!"

He grabbed a sweater, pulled it around his shoulders, and set off for the park. The weather was no cold, only slightly chilly. The sweater was more of a protection from things coming into his life than a blanket to ward off the morning chill.

When he arrived at his usual bench he sat down. "It feels good to have something solid beneath me." For a time he was almost avoiding the questions that had been uppermost in his thinking all morning. He stared off into space, unaware of what was before him. Workmen, passing through before him, greeted him with their "Good morning!" but he shut them out. They had turned on the water for sprinkling the grass and plants. Drops of water hit his face and clothing, but he didn't seem to notice or to care.

There came a moment when Martin felt the hardness of the concrete bench. "Why am I feeling the hardness of this bench? I was looking for something solid, but this is so unmoving. It doesn't give to me what I need to hear or need to feel. What is the message? Bench, what are you trying to tell me? Why am I not sensing he joy that I felt yesterday and on Wednesday, just before the cloudburst? Talk to me, bench. Are you like everything else about me, unwilling to share what you want me to hear?"

"I'm hungry. What do I want? What food will satisfy my craving?" Martin got up from the bench and walked to the little restaurant where he had eaten a couple of days earlier. He was pleased to find that there was almost no one else in the restaurant. He really didn't want to talk with anyone.

A waitress came to his table. "May I help you, sir? What would you like?"

He thought to himself, "I'd like some answers to these questions that keep bugging me." She would never understand. "Wow, what an important, simple question! 'May I help you?' Oh, if only someone could. 'What would you like?' I'd like peace. I'd like to get rid of the things in my memory that will not let me go. That's what I'd like."

"What's your special today?" He asked.

"We have omelets. There are many things we can include in your omelet. You'll have to decide if you want a two egg, a three egg, or we could make you one with a dozen eggs. You make a choice."

"Do I have to choose? Why don't you surprise me? In twenty years it won't matter. In fact it probably doesn't matter now."

"Now why did I do that? Omelet, what are you saying to me? Why did I have the waitress decide what combination you'll be when they bring you to me? And I thought coming to this 'hole-in- the-wall' restaurant would help me escape those disturbing questions! Help me, help me! Can anyone or anything help me? What am I supposed to learn?"

Martin ate his omelet. There was something unsatisfying about the breakfast. He thanked the waitress, left money for the breakfast and a tip, and made his way back to his apartment.

Once more he faced the sterile qualities of his room. An awareness was beginning to come to him, although he didn't fully understand what was happening. Still bothered by what had happened, he was only more determined not to let go of the questions that plagued him. "I'll stay with whatever is going on within me until I am told what it is about."

All day long, his memory kept playing moments in his history. They were disturbing events, events that were as unsatisfying as the three egg omelet with ham and cheese at breakfast. The day wore on. He would not let go. It was a painful time. It was a time, which for some reason, must be played out in his mind. He was unsure of why it had to be.

Exhausted from the struggles of the day, Martin undressed and went to bed. He drew the covers up around his neck as if attempting to protect himself from what had played upon him all day. He was not sure just when he finally dozed off into a deep sleep.

It was some time after three in the morning that Martin became aware of ideas forming in his mind. A song began at some level of his consciousness. It was as if the ideas must come from the very depth of his being, that some message must be related to, and come from, the awakening of his soul. The melody was rich and vibrant. He heard these words: "Come sweet sounds, come and bless these days. Know that we are yours, now and for always." The music stopped. The sound of his own voice spoke clearly, "Martin, you cannot hide. You are intelligent. Call upon that mind to serve you. You are only called to be as authentic at this moment, as you can be, and to give as much of yourself to others as you are free to give and they are free to receive."

With all of that he turned his body away from the light. He drew the sheet about his body and fell deeply into sleep.

When he awakened the sun was shining. Light filled the room. "It's Saturday morning. Saturday morning? I'll be late for the breakfast!" With a rush, he threw back the covers, sprang from his bed, and rushed to the bathroom for those early morning activities. He quickly brushed his teeth, shaved, combed his hair, and in haste, dressed for the morning. He was rushing from his apartment, buttoning the sleeves of his shirt as he went.

Chapter 8

At the breakfast

Martin raced across the park and hurriedly entered the basement of the church.

"Good to see you, Martin. Were the covers heavy last night? Whatever! I'm pleased you're here. I want you to meet some of your neighbors," Dr. Bonner said as she wheeled herself to the group assembled away from the entrance to the basement dining room. She began the introductions.

Martin was standing with his back to the entrance way when he heard a familiar voice,

"Mitch Roberts, am I happy to see you!"

Martin froze in place. It was the voice of Mr. James, owner of Supreme Food Products. "What do I do now? How can this happen to me? What does he think of my leaving his company? I'd like to get lost. How can I disappear?" he thought.

Mr. James came rushing over. He turned Martin around, shaking his hand, with a smile that stretched across his face. "You'll never guess who came to my office a couple of days ago. Randal Garrett of the A and P Company. He asked about you. He was intrigued by your ideas of how A and P could market Supreme Food Products. He wanted to talk with you some more, but couldn't find you."

Martin was amazed. He stood speechless.

Mr. James continued. "We want you back with the company. When you left, we began a search for someone to do our marketing. We couldn't find anyone with your qualifications. I want you back. There is one condition. You must have an office at our headquarters. I want to benefit from your insights. I want all our employees to get to know you and to benefit from your thinking."

Martin turned away from Mr. James. What would he think about a grown man crying, as tears wet his face? "Excuse me, Mr. James." He walked away to the Men's Room to dry his eyes and compose himself before returning.

Mr. James continued the conversation. "I realize this is something you may want to think about. Know that we want you back and we feel you can play a most important part in our company." Mr. James shook Martin's hand again before turning to assist in the preparations of the breakfast.

Martin found a spot at the table and seated himself beside a gentleman from the neighborhood. "Good morning, friend. I'm Martin Roberts. I suspect you have a name."

"I'm Ray Wynn," came the reply.

"From around here? Is this where you first saw the light of day? What do you do?"

"I came here from far away, California. I am an artist. I once had a very good job doing art for a company. We were doing very well. Then I became ill. I could no longer do the art. The company found another artist and I became homeless. It is through the good work of Dr. Bonner that I am able to survive. That woman is a saint."

Martin listened carefully.

"I watch her serve from her wheelchair. She is amazing. She would never admit to a handicap. Why would I complain for what has been given me? I trust something will seek me out," Ray continued.

Just then they began serving the omelets, each one unique to the choices made by individuals coming to breakfast. Martin watched Ray consume his food. As he leaned over to assist him with his breakfast, he caught a whiff of the body odors. Obviously, showers were in short supply. He glanced at the man's tattered clothes and the beard of several days that punctuated the lines of his face. "What does this man need?" Martin asked himself.

The conversation turned to talking about the taste of the food and the work of students from Lily Wong's Cooking School who had prepared the omelets. That was a comfortable topic to pass the time.

When the breakfast was over, Martin turned to Ray and said, "Would you be offended if I invited you to come to my apartment about noon? I have a tiny bathroom. Some say it's so small you have to step outside to change your mind. You could enjoy a shower. I do have some clothes that I think would fit you. I was about to give them away, but if they would fit you then it would save me having to find an agency to take them. After that I'd really like to have you join me at a 'little-hole-in-the-wall restaurant' for lunch. Interested?"

"Haven't had a better offer today. You say about noon? How can I find your apartment?"

"It's in the apartment building on the other side of the park. My place is on the second floor. Do plan to come." Ray bid Martin goodbye, thanking him for the invitation.

Dr. Bonner had been watching the conversation from the other side of the room. She could not hear what was being said, but the expressions on their faces revealed something of the essence. They were beginning to open up to each other.

"Well, Mr. Goodguy. That was a most impressive discussion, at least from what I imagined while watching the two of you, Are you ready for that talk? Why don't you go on up to my office and wait for me? I have some things to finish with Mr. James, and then I'll be there. Don't read all the books in my library."

Dr. Bonner whirled her chair around and went dashing off to find Mr. James. Martin thoughtfully made his way to her office.

Chapter 9

A New Beginning

Martin thoughtfully left the dining room and went directly to Dr. Bonner's office. It was an awesome experience to be among the things that represented this person becoming a special friend. He glanced at the books in the library. There was the urge to explore the contents of the books. Much of him was caught up in how to share with her what had been happening to him. How would he begin the conversation? Would she understand the importance of what he was sharing with her? Would she be able to hear what it was all about? Would he be able to share with her his growing feelings for her? The questions kept racing through his mind. While the books on the shelf promised answers to questions, there were questions yet unformed in his mind. He waited anxiously.

"Well, I see you are alive and well." Dr. Bonner began. "I was watching you during the breakfast. I was especially interested in what was happening between you and Ray Wynn. Are you the same guy that, with utmost speed, brought me to the church to avoid raindrops?"

He whirled around with a grin on his face as he looked at Dr. Bonner. "Now look at what you have unleashed. So much has happened since the cloudburst. I hardly know where to begin."

"Start with whatever seems strongest in your experience. If I don't understand I'll simply ask some questions."

"Wednesday was an amazing day for me. It began with my wanting to be alone but not to be alone. The rain began. You wheeled yourself my way as the raindrops began to increase. Those raindrops awakened me. Then I heard you say, 'Sir, would you help me across the street to my office?' Someone needed me! We went racing across the street like a couple of kids playing a game. The cloudburst made me captive in your building."

"I do remember that. It was threatening and fun at the same time. I'm so grateful for your coming to my rescue. Please continue."

"Since it was raining so hard and I couldn't leave, you invited me to push you to your office. I knew you could do that yourself, but I suspect you used that as a ploy to get to know me better."

"Those classes at Ohio State must have had a great impact on you, to know something of the 'why' I provided an invitation. Go on."

"That was Wednesday. On Thursday I went to the park, hoping that you'd return. I sat there but you didn't come. I suddenly felt like a ten year old and the bullies of my fourth grade class taunting me with, 'Here comes smarty Marty, Wants to join our party! Come on, guys, let's run and hide,' and I felt a kind of loneliness that I have felt often in my life. But you did return and invited me to breakfast on Saturday morning."

"I do remember. You were reluctant. You tried to find a way not to come to that neighborhood gathering where you could meet some of your neighbors."

"That was very threatening. But I trusted you. Although it was not in my comfort zone, I agreed to come. I thought to myself, 'Now Martin, what have you let yourself in for?'.

"Something within me seemed to cry out for a presence in my life. The night was tormenting. I tossed and turned the whole night long. Something would not let go of me.

"Things I would choose not to talk about kept coming into my consciousness. Those fourth grade bullies kept reappearing. My relationship, or the lack of it, with my wife, with whom I am now separated, the pictures of her teaching our son Jack the skills of sports, the rejection of my application for president of Supreme Food Products, my getting drunk and missing seeing my son off to service, all these memories kept flooding in upon me. I had the feeling they were trying to tell me something.

"Then about three in the morning somewhere in my mind, I heard the beginnings of a song."

Martin sang the melody, "Come sweet sounds. Come and bless our days. We are yours, now and for always." The song ended abruptly. "I heard my own voice talking to me, 'Martin, you cannot hide. You are intelligent. Use that mind to solve your problems You are only called to be as authentic, at this moment, as you can be, and to give as much of yourself to others, as you are free to give and they are free to receive.'

"An incredible peace came over me. It had been a long time since sleep had been so wonderful. I almost slept through your neighborhood breakfast meeting."

"I was aware of your lateness in arriving. I also remember I was introducing you to some of the neighbors when Mr. James shouted out, 'Mitch Roberts! How wonderful to see you!' He came rushing over, turned you around and warmly shook your hand. Then I heard him say, 'You'll never guess who stopped by my office. Randall Garrett of the A and P Company came by wanting to see you. He said he wanted to talk about ideas you had shared earlier, or something like that. Then Mr. James said he wanted you back with the company, but that must be your decision. He wanted you to have an office near his offices that he might share ideas with you."

"That was an awesome experience. When I heard his voice, I froze. 'What would he want of me? How would I relate to him after being turned down from my wanting to be president? His warm greeting and the invitation to come back to work was so comforting.

"I remember your saying that we had to make a choice of what we wanted in our omelets, that life is filled with the requirements of making choices. I looked at the long list of options and decided to be conservative and have only two eggs instead of three but to be adventurous and have everything, all the ingredients, in my omelet. "I found a place at the table. I sat beside a gentleman who was obviously impoverished. His clothes were very worn and his body odors stated baths were in short supply. I asked his name. He said, 'Ray Wynn'. I asked him what he was most interested in. He answered, 'I am an artist. I once did promotional art work for a major company. Then I became very ill and could not do the work. I was dismissed. I am unemployed.'

"I told him I had some clothes that I was going to take to an agency and I thought they might fit him. He could have them if they fit. I don't know why I made that offer? I also said I had a bathroom with a shower and, although it was so small he would have to step outside it to change his mind, I'd like him to come use it. Then we'd go out for lunch, unless he had a better offer. He said, 'It's the best offer I've had today.' I told him how to find my apartment and that he should come by a little before noon."

"What an amazing story! I would love for all people to have such a deep experience. It is as if it is coming from the depth of your soul," Dr. Bonner added.

"Dr. Bonner," he began.

"I think we can use our names. The other sounds too formal. Please call me Beatrice."

"Thank you, Beatrice. I am so comfortable when I'm with you. You seem to anticipate my needs and know how I can begin to find myself.

"Thursday, when I didn't see you, I felt so alone. The image of myself as a ten year old returned. I saw those bullies in my fourth grade class that taunted me with their jingle. That image kept coming back in my consciousness on Friday. How can I get rid of those memories?"

"Tell me more about your earliest years. What was life like in your home?"

"I have the most wonderful parents. My mother was a kindergarten teacher and my father was the principal of the high school. From my earliest days they spent time with my learning.

Even before I had words to express myself, when we went to the library, they would take me to the section for children and we'd explore books with pictures. I'd take many books home to 'study'. When I found words to express myself, I'd look at the pictures and make up stories the pictures seemed to tell. Then often I'd get to choose a story book and take it to my father, and I'd crawl up on his lap and he'd read the story to me. Sometimes, when I was very familiar with the story, he'd invent a new ending, just to get me to correct him. I'd say, 'No, no, no! That's not the way it goes.' He'd say, 'Dear me, I've forgotten how it goes. Can you tell me how it ends?' and I'd end the story as I had remembered it. I now know he was helping me develop my memory and my language. I have always devoured books."

"So that's the roots of the 'Smarty Marty' events when you were in fourth grade? What did you do when the bullies tried to get the best of you?"

`"Many times I'd try to play dumb. I'd pretend I didn't know the answer to a question asked by the teacher. It never worked for me. I couldn't wait to read a source that answered the question with the greatest depth possible."

"I'd like you to tell me the story again. Begin with your being where the bullies enter. Tell me the story as best you remember it. I want you .to imagine this as being a tape recording of the event. Play all the parts."

"I'm standing outside the building, excited about another day at school. Suddenly I see those five guys with their leader, Bruce. They spot me, and they get in a huddle. They break up and begin singing, 'Here comes smarty Marty. Wants to join our party. Come on, guys, let's run and hide."

"Stop the tape. I want you to splice a new ending to that story. How would you like that story to end?"

"Bruce needs help. I'd like to find a way of helping him become a better student.

"I'd go on into the school and watch them see me departing without responding to their actions. I wouldn't want to empower them. Then, in school, there is a very difficult problem in math. Bruce needs help. I'd go to him and help him see how the problem is solved. He thanks me for my help. Eventually we become very close friends."

"The process you've just gone through is called neuro-linguistic programming. You cannot change what happened long ago but you can change the intent of the event and how you would like it to end."

"Then I can create new endings to all those stories that plague me?"

"It is one means to wholeness. A difficult part is being able to forgive ourselves for the problems that we are a part of. Asking forgiveness of others' hurt is a step in the right direction. Forgiving oneself is often the more difficult task. Owning a problem is a vital step. If the problems own us, it is very difficult to let go of it."

"Thank you, Dr. - Thank you, Beatrice. I need to get back to my apartment, to be there when Ray Wynn drops by. I think I have some clothes that will fit him. Then, I must meet with Mr. James to discuss his invitation to return to my marketing job.

"Your breakfast neighborhood meeting was far more than I could have expected. Who knows where those relationships will lead us." Martin moved toward Beatrice as if to make physical contact but stopped short, not knowing how to relate with her at some closer level. He bid her goodbye and walked away from the building, across the park and back to his apartment.

Chapter 10

Finding Fresh Beginnings

The struggles of Friday, the Saturday early morning awakening, the breakfast events, and the session with Beatrice echoed in his mind. He heard again, "You cannot hide. All you are asked to do is to be as authentic as you can be, and to give as much of yourself as you are free to give and others are free to receive."

"What a mess this room is. What clothes will fit Ray? Do I have extra underwear? Where's an extra towel? It's almost noon and I'm not ready. Heaven help me!"

Just then there was a rap at the door. Martin quickly walked to the door opening it. "Welcome to my humble abode. It's not much, but what is here can be shared."

Ray smiled without saying a word, entered the room. "Looks like a palace to me!"

"I'll lay out some clothes while you shower. Here's a towel and some clean underwear. When you're out we can look at the clothes."

Ray removed his clothes, throwing them into a pile on the floor. His nakedness displayed the very bone structure of his body. It revealed the lack of food. His shaggy beard hid the lines on his face.

"Get in that shower. I'll have some things for you to try on when you get out." As Martin listened to the water in the shower, he thought of the downpour that provided the time together with

Beatrice. "Does water have magic within it?" he thought to himself. Very soon Ray emerged with the towel wrapped around his middle. "Want to shave that beard, Ray?" Martin asked. "If I do that and look myself in the mirror I may not know myself."

"I think it's worth the chance. But then, that's your choice."

"Bring on the razor. I'll risk it!" With a few swipes, his face shed its whiskers.

"Man! What an improvement. Now start trying on these duds!" Ray soon settled on a pair of pants, a shirt, and a casual jacket that Martin often wore to play golf.

"Has all of this given you an appetite? I'm hungry! Let's move it!" Martin stated as they headed toward the door. Martin picked up a tablet with blank pages and some pencils that he often used while sketching ideas with clients, as they stepped into the hallway.

They made their way down the stairs, across the street, through the park and to the restaurant. Martin led the way, finding a table and parking himself looking toward the window at the front of the room. The light shone fully on his face.

"Aren't you the dude that was here yesterday?" the waitress asked. "I remember you. You only picked at your food. I thought then, 'he'll never come back, but here you are. What's your name? Who's your friend?"

"I was here yesterday. It was a terrible day. This is a new friend, Ray Wynn." Ray had spotted the tablet and pencils and had begun a drawing of Martin.

"How amazing," the waitress said looking at the drawing. Then calling to others she said, "Hey, guys, you gotta see this. This guy's something else. Look, with just a few lines he's captured the feeling of this other guy. Amazing! Would you do a drawing of me? I'll pay you for it."

For a time all service in the restaurant ended. Everyone gathered about Ray. Even some of the customers left their meals to watch what was taking place.

The manager became engaged, "May I remind you people we

have a restaurant to run. Back on your jobs." The customers stayed observing Ray as he drew.

One customer spoke with excitement in his voice, "Man, you have a great talent. I'd like to have you do a portrait of me. I'll pay you for it."

"I need to get better paper and more pens to do the job right. I'll come back tomorrow at lunch time. We could do your picture then. Thank you for the request," Ray said.

Lights began flashing in the manager's mind. "If people would come to have their portrait made, perhaps I should advertise his work. We could hang pictures of important people who come to eat here. This could be a bonanza. He spoke directly to Ray, "Sir, I'd be most pleased to have you come and do pictures of people. I might even set up an easel in the front window so people walking by would come in to watch you. And then, of course, stay on for lunch. We could make it worth your while if you'd be willing to come."

"Best offer I've had in days"

Martin interrupted, "Ray you haven't even ordered your lunch. I know there are artists that would rather draw or paint, than eat." They did order. The waitress especially cared for Ray's order. When lunch was over Martin began, "I best get my car and drive you to where you live."

Ray was silent.

"Where do you live, Ray?" Martin asked.

"It's okay. I'll find my own way."

"What are you trying to tell me? What is this all about?"

"To be honest, I sleep where ever I can find a place. Thank you for all you've done for me today. I'll be alright."

"Sleeping wherever you can find a place? Not in my book you don't. I was to meet Mr. James to talk about my returning to the company. That can wait. Right now we're going to a second hand store to look for a roll-away bed. There's not a lot of room in my apartment but there is room for one more bed. That is my decision. There is no other alternative. You are about to be my roommate."

As they made their way out of the restaurant, Martin heard, in his mind, the words revealed in the early morning hour, "Be as authentic as you can be. Give of as much of yourself to others as you are free to give and they are free to receive."

Chapter 11

Beginning Again

Martin, having gotten a roll-a-way bed and taken Ray back to his apartment, excused himself, and hopped in his car to drive to the Supreme Food Products administrative offices. Parking his car, he rushed to the suite with Mr. James' Private Office on the door.

"Good afternoon, Miss Franks."

"You remembered my name!"

"Not knowing a person's name is a bad practice. Not knowing it at two meetings in a row is the worst. Even though Supreme Food Products is about foods, one shouldn't end up with 'egg on his face'."

"I know Mr. James is expecting you, Mr. Roberts. He seemed excited about your coming in for a meeting with him. His son, the president of Supreme Foods, is with him at the moment. If you can wait, I'm sure Mr. James will see you momentarily."

Martin had hardly gotten seated when the door to Mr. James office opened and the father and son stepped forward to shake hands. "Mitch, or do we call you Martin now? I don't remember introducing you to my son Leland. He is just leaving."

"Please stay. What I have to say, your being president of the company, you might find of interest."

The three men returned to Mr. James' office.

Mr. James began the conversation. "Have you given thought, Martin, to the invitation to return to Supreme Foods?"

Martin glanced about the office. He began seeing things he didn't remember seeing when he was last there. His eyes circled the room. His attention stopped at the large picture of a family gathered together. He walked to the picture. "And who are these people?"

Mr. James brightened. "That's my family, taken years ago."

"And are you in it?" Martin asked.

"See the child on Grandmother James' lap? That's me. I was the first grandchild. The event must have been an important one. All nine children of Grandmother James were there. Many of my father's brothers and sisters, my aunts and uncles, had their husbands, wives, boyfriends or girlfriends there for the event."

"I don't see an older man, possibly your grandfather?" Martin continued.

"That's part of this incredible story. My grandparents lived on a very large farm between here and Baronsville. They had a large herd of milk cows. During the day, the herd was turned out to graze in the pastures. At each milking, so I'm told, my grandfather would hop on the back of his favorite mare and they'd go fetch the cows. They said he never used a saddle and never bridled the horse. To give directions to his mare he'd simply lean in the direction to be taken, or grasping the mane, would move it 'gee' or 'haw' and the horse would respond to his direction. On one such day, something spooked the horse, and she reared up, throwing my grandfather to the ground. He landed, so I'm told, head down and broke his neck. They didn't find him immediately, but when they did find him he was dead.

"This left my grandmother with nine children. My father was the eldest. He became the 'man' of the house. It was his job to do most of the field and farm work. As a teenager that was demanding. But he grew up not fearing work.

"A most amazing thing happened in those days. All the neighbors pitched in and gave so much support to my grandmother and her family. The neighboring men would advise my father on how to do certain things he had not yet learned. The ladies of the church had bake sales to raise money for the things grandmother couldn't raise on the farm by herself. I'm told the family never went hungry because they had a large garden that the younger children tended. All summer long, vegetables and meats were canned for use in the winter.

Grandfather James had planted an orchard of apple, peach and cherry trees. Each in their season were picked and processed. The fruits were shared among the people of the neighborhood. Am I boring you?"

"Heavens, no! Would that we might experience such things today!" Martin quickly replied.

Mr. James continued. "The cows were milked morning and evening each day. The milk was sold to raise some money. The farm had a cream separator. Cream was separated from the milk. That cream became a marvelous topping for Grandmother James' pies. Some of it was churned into sweet butter which grandmother shared with her friends. Everyone looked forward to getting some of her sweet butter.

"Grandmother's cooking and the material produced on the farm grew in great demand. Neighbors wanted her things enough they were willing to pay her for them. My father and his brothers and sisters not only had to run the farm, but soon began to deliver things made from the farm. It was the very generation of Supreme Food Products. But let us get back to you and your returning to our company. Have you given thought to returning to Supreme Foods?"

Martin began, "The story of your family is most impressive. I loved how they solved their family problems. I'm not sure of how I might fit into such a pattern.

"My memory of our last meeting in this office is painful, not because of what you said, but the manner in which I responded. It was my intense desire to be president of your company. It was a disaster. I am now attempting to eliminate those memories from my mind. I am finding help from Dr. Bonner at your church. I am aware that something within me is changing.

"I do believe I know something about marketing. There is much I do not know about other parts of the company. Your conditional invitation to return to the vice-presidency with an office here in the company headquarters may help with that matter. I don't know how that will play out. Because of what I'm discovering about myself with Beatrice - Dr. Bonner, I believe I must get inside the matter to discover how I might function.

"I will accept the invitation for a six months period. I need to know that what I do empowers all within the organization."

"Great!" Mr. James replied. "We'll begin by introducing you to each of the department heads in the company. It is the dedication of the employees that signal success for our company. You need to know them and they need to know you. On your first day back we'll begin the introductions. The custodial staff will be setting up your office. We do know the effect of Beatrice Bonner and her work. She has a positive impact on the members of the church and the community around the church. It was my grandfather, a farmer, a carpenter, and a cabinet maker that began the church. There is furniture in the church that Grandfather James made with his own hands. As a matter of fact, the desk in my office was made by him. His neighbors often told that, when planing the wood, he would rub his hand over the wood, not to test its smoothness, but to caressing it into being"

"Yes, I want to be here. I will do my best to make things work. Earlier today I met a homeless man at the breakfast meeting, Ray Wynn, an artist." Was that just today? How could so much happen in such a short time?

"I purchased a roll-away-bed to have him share my one room apartment. I must get back and help him create a dinner for the two of us. The revealing of his ribs on his flesh-starved body tells me food from Supreme Foods is necessary. I'll begin on Monday. Thank you for sharing this time." Martin grabbed his hat and headed out the door. "Goodbye. Miss Franks. See you Monday!"

Mr. James and son Leland looked at each other and smiled. A nod of their heads said much about their belief that the invitation was the right thing to do.

Martin stopped at a grocery store to purchase food for their dinner. "A steak would be a most appropriate means of celebrating all that has happened this day." He would have to think about what would go well with two T-bones. Off to the grocery and the meat market.

Ray was fully dressed and had their little table set for their dinner. When Martin opened the door, with his arms filled with sacks of food, Ray rushed to him, taking the sacks and setting them on the table. "What have you been doing this afternoon, Ray?"

"I went back to the restaurant. That cute waitress gave me a down payment for her picture. I went to an office supply store and purchased some quality art paper and some other things I needed. I went back and did a portrait of her. Wow! She's something else. If other could see what I saw as I drew her, she wouldn't just be waiting tables at that restaurant. But then not all can see the beauty within a person. I got several more orders from people who came to the restaurant. I'm ready to celebrate this day. What is the passage to this celebration?"

"T-bone steaks, corn-on-the-cob, and a Supreme Food chocolate cake with the stamp of approval of Grandmother James written all over it. What did I just say?" He thought to himself,

"Keep that thought in your brain, Martin. That may be of value one of these days." The dinner was a glorious success in spite of the problem of cooking it with limited cookware. Was it because of the food itself, or was there something that sharpened the taste? After dinner, Ray took charge of clearing the table and doing the dishes. Martin sank into the one soft chair in the room. "We must get another chair or two, Ray. If this room is going to take on the splendor it's destined to become, we must help it in its destiny. Life, as I am beginning to learn from Dr. Bonner is, in part, what we help it to be."

The two men shared their joy as they talked about so much happening in such a short time. They turned out the lights. The street light shone through the slit in the shade and left its mark on the wall. Each crawled into his own bed and was soon sound asleep. Was this just Saturday?

Chapter 12

Going to Church?

This Sunday was to be unlike any before in most of Martin's life. Not since his marriage to Gladys had he ever darkened the doors of a church. Church? When golf was so inviting? And there was the promise of becoming president of Supreme Foods waiting if he showed real business ability?

Ray was the first to awaken. "I'll race you to the bathroom! Get up you sleepy head! I'm seeing you get to church this morning."

"Go on! When you've finished you can get out the cereal and the milk. I'm ready for forty more winks!" Martin turned his body away from the light and drew his covers up around his head to shut out the light.

Ray began singing, "Eency weency spider went up the water spout. Down came the rain and washed the spider out. Out came the sun and dried up all the rain, and the eency weency spider went up the spout again."

Martin pulled the covers over his ears. "Can't we remember any song except those we learned when we were kids?" he thought to himself as he tried to shut out the sounds of water spraying in the shower. "Oh yes, now I remember, the cloudburst and my meeting Dr. Bonner." The thought caused him to stir, throw back the covers and pull himself into a sitting position at the side of his bed. "I wonder what Beatrice does in the morning? How does she manage all the details of her day, getting the braces on, attending to her morning rituals, getting breakfast, getting to her car and driving to the church? Why is my mind given to so much thought about this woman? It was only five days ago the torrential rainstorm brought us together. How could so much happen in such a short time?

She would probably say that it was all waiting to be revealed to me. I was ready for change! But how does it work? I must talk that over with her sometime in the future. I wonder what she's doing at this very moment."

Martin destined his head for the pillow. He tried to go back to sleep but the memories of the past days kept racing through his mind. He pulled the covers over his head to shut out the light. It didn't work. Nothing would support his unneeded need for sleep.

As he sat there at the side of his bed, Ray emerged dressed in boxer shorts and a towel slung over his shoulder. "Now that was refreshing. A nice cool shower is guaranteed to get that blood stirring." He flipped the towel on Martin's legs. "Time to move, friend! We don't want to be late this morning. I won't tell you what. It'll be a surprise. I guarantee you'll like it."

Martin stood for a moment beside his bed as if to be sure his body was able to function. He grabbed a dry towel, clean underwear, and headed for the bathroom. "No Eency, Weency Spider for me. Good grief, what time is it?" Peaking out the door he added, "The street lights are off. Lift the shade and let the daylight in. I'd better hurry."

The morning rituals were quickly mastered. Ray had the cereal bowls, the cereal, and the milk on the table when Martin exhumed himself from the cramped space called a bathroom. Imitating Ray he then exclaimed, "Well, Chef Wynn, what marvelous morsels have you prepared for this starving character by the name of Martin Roberts?"

"I'm pleased to inform you, Master Roberts, I had flown in from the corn fields of Iowa, the most delicious corn that has ever been produced for the Kellogg factories in Michigan. And, the milk is from the supreme cows of the Supreme Food Products Company. The sugar was produced in the cane fields of Hawaii especially for you. Now get your butt in gear, get it over here, and be of good cheer."

"Thank you Mr. Longfellow. You're a poet! We didn't know it. Now don't you blow it! It's the action, you have to show it! No toast today?"

"Don't we have to have bread to make toast?"

"Always something -never satisfied! You'd think we were made of money!" The two grown men were having so much fun playing a game like kids. "Wait 'til I share with Dr. Bonner this episode. She won't believe it. How can two grown men have so much fun?" he thought to himself.

Breakfast was soon history. "Chef Wynn," Martin continued, "I congratulate you on this marvelous feast. Without question it is the finest breakfast I've had today!"

Ray retorted, "Very punny! Very punny! Get your bod' in gear and get dressed for church."

Ray once more cleared the table and washed the dishes and silverware. In no time they had dressed and headed down the stairs, across the street and the park to the church.

The organ prelude had already begun when they entered the sanctuary. It was a marvelous improvisation on a familiar hymn, unknown to Martin but fully known by Ray. But then how does one learn hymns while on a golf course? The music swelled to a dramatic climax and then in contrast brought a softness to the piece. Only the sound of the melody line played on a solo 4 foot flute stop brought the music to its end. All was quiet and relaxed. The people in the congregation had responded to the drama of the music and in the end a prayerful response,

Martin was aware suddenly that a wheelchair had entered the chancel. In the chair was Dr. Beatrice Bonner. The memories of the past five days quickened his pulse upon seeing her. She wheeled herself to the pulpit, then, locking the wheels on her chair, adjusted her braces and stood behind the pulpit just as a ray of sunlight peered through the stained glass window and shown like a halo on her golden blond hair. It was as if an artist, in a moment of magic, had captured her beauty to be remembered for all times.

She began, "Dr. Phillips, our pastor, is on a study tour to the holy lands. I think that today's he's in the ancient city of Corinth, reliving the mission of Paul. Please be in a prayerful mood as you hear this call to worship."

Timothy Cole, a teenager, began a written prayer. "Please join me in our prayer of invitation. 'God, creator of all in the universe, for the grandeur of the galaxies to the beauty of the smallest of flowers, all in perfection, we give thanks for this day and the opportunity to serve in your name. Amen."

The organist began with the introduction to "Love Divine, All Loves Excelling." Many of the congregation didn't bother to open their hymnals, so familiar were they with the song. "Love divine, all love excelling, Joy of heaven to earth, come down;" Everyone sang with warmth and conviction to the very end.

Beatrice, standing again, turned to the organist and said, "Okay, Earl, step up that beat. I wanna dance!" As on cue, he doubled the tempo as Dr. Bonner snapped her fingers, tossed her head, and responded to the beat.

"You're probably wondering why I wanted to dance? With this body? When I was a small child, whenever music played, I danced. Then at age seven, I contracted polio. I was at the edge of death for days. They weren't sure I would survive. I was loved back to life by my family. A part of me wondered why I was condemned to this disease. I felt sorry for myself. Then I read a book about a young dancer. It was filled with the most descriptive ballet dance movements. My mother took me to meet the author. I made my way to the front of the audience to await the author's entry. As she entered, I turned to see her confined to a wheel chair, with a body terribly distorted.

"There was a gasp from the audience. One woman boldly asked, 'How could you ever write such a beautiful story of a dancing girl when your body is so locked up?'

"The author replied simply and lovingly, 'I've danced my whole life. What you see is what a body does. A dance begins inside oneself. I've been blessed with the ability to experience dance from within my body, within my soul! When I feel the movement! The writing is easy.'

"I never forgot that truth. It is not only dance that begins inside, and most of the important things in life must have their origins from deep inside oneself. I was blessed with being loved by my family and friends. I heard affirmation for each new step I was taking. With the affirmation and love, I learned to trust, first with those about me and later to trust myself. As I learned to trust, I was willing to risk. As I took risks and heard affirmation, I trusted more, took more risks and became more whole. An important realization was that my growth was my responsibility. No one could solve my problems. One of my favorite teachers who lived almost two thousand years ago tried to teach us much of this truth. What is our responsibility? Affirmation and unconditional acceptance, or love, costs little but pays high dividends. Is it possible that we each can affirm each other and express our caring? What might happen in this community if that were to happen? How can we begin?

"That teacher also told stories to help us learn, just as we tell each other stories today. Only today we don't call them parables, even though that's what they are. Parables are stories.

"Have you ever wanted something so much that you gave your all to it, only in the end to not be able to achieve it or if it happened, there was an emptiness with having it? That tale is told over and over as we give our energies to something other than a deeper truth within us. Think for a moment of something that happened in your life that resulted in a feeling of emptiness." Dr. Bonner paused, giving members of the congregation a moment to reflect.

"Do I know that story?" Martin thought, then glancing across the congregation, saw Mr. James. A moment of despair rose in his mind, but then he dismissed it.

Dr. Bonner continued. "There is this marvelous parable about a family that had two sons. The one son asked his father to divide the inheritance, and give him his share. This the father did. That son took his inheritance and went to a city far from the family's farm. There he lived a frivolous life, eating, drinking, having women entertain him, until all his money was spent. He took a job doing the least menial work. He longed for the days on his father's farm.

"He thought, 'I'll go home and ask to be a servant. I've made wrong choices and now I must pay the piper.' He began the long, painful journey home. A servant saw him coming and told the father. His father raced out to meet him, throwing his arms about him, tears of joy streaming down his cheeks. The father called to the servants, 'Get the finest robe and rings for his fingers. Get the fatted calf. Prepare it for a feast. My son was dead but lives again.'

"That story was filled with unconditional acceptance or love. The son was able to confess his error, and he owned his condition. He wanted to change his life, a willingness to change, or in church terms, to repent. He received forgiveness from the father. I often wonder how he was able to forgive himself. It is often easier to experience forgiveness from another than to forgive oneself. The story tells about the elder brother's response, but nothing about how the younger son lived his renewal and reconciliation. Is that because there is no one way to express renewal? Are we each to use the gifts given us to empower those with whom we share our lives?

"As a psychologist and an employee of this church, I find it interesting the parallel between the psychological and the theological factors leading to wholeness.

"I've invited Ray Wynn, a faithful member of our church, to read the story of the 'Prodigal Son'."

One of the homeless who attended the neighborhood breakfast on Saturday thought, "Is that Ray? Doesn't look like the guy who had breakfast with us yesterday!"

Ray rose from his seat and made his way to the chancel. He read with warmth and conviction. When he came to the end of the reading, he closed the Bible and facing the congregation said, "I know this is not a part of the planned service but I feel compelled to share what has happened in my life in a little more than twenty-four hours. You will remember that students from Lily Wong's Cooking School served us an omelet breakfast. Seated beside me at breakfast was a new-found friend, Martin Roberts. Until this morning he said he almost never attended a church service. He invited me to come to his one-room apartment to shower and try on some clothes he said he was going to give away. Then he took me to lunch. For some unknown reason he took along an unlined tablet and some pens. Being an artist, I was drawn to sketching what I saw in Martin, something that is known only in the soul of a person. The waitress was fascinated by my work. In no time she had called others to watch what I was doing. She wanted me to make a drawing of her and she would pay me for. Soon I was filled with requests for my drawings. The manager of the restaurant has invited me to draw pictures of others.

"Then an amazing thing happened. Martin wanted to drive me to where I lived. I had to confess that I had slept for the last few months where ever I could find a place. He said he had an appointment with Mr. James but that could wait, that we were going to a second hand store looking for a roll-away-bed. His one-room apartment was like a palace to me. What did the Prodigal Son do following being brought back into his family? The scriptures do not say. Did he look for a roll-away-bed for someone in need? I feel most blessed for a breakfast and for a new friendship. As a Prodigal Son, I must find a way to serve others."

Ray bowed his head as if to give thanks. He returned to his seat beside Martin Roberts.

Mr. James took note of his disclosure. A beautiful waitress from the restaurant smiled, knowing she had been a part of his supporting 'family'.

Following the benediction and the organ postlude, Dr. Bonner made her way to the narthex to greet people as they left. Mr. James waited for Martin and Ray, and then, warmly grasping their hands, said to Martin, "I'll see you early tomorrow morning. We should have an office space ready." Turning to Ray, he said, "Thank you for the gift you gave. By the way, what would it cost me to have you do a portrait of me?" Not waiting for a reply, Mr. James departed, greeting Dr. Bonner, thanking her for the morning service. "You are really a dancer, in my book!" He was gone.

Chapter 13

Returning to Supreme Foods

Martin squinted his eyes to look at the clock. "Only 4:00 A.M.? Why am I getting awake so early? Why am I looking forward to this day? Isn't it the same job I've done for many years?" Even though he had done marketing for over twenty years, he was feeling like a young man on his very first date, excited about the possibilities but anxious to make the right impression.

He looked over at Ray, snoring away. "I wonder what time he got in?" Martin thought. "I looked at the clock at ten thirty and he wasn't in yet. Wasn't he going to begin an oil painting of the waitress from the restaurant? Could a sitting and art work last that long? Or is there something else going on they haven't told me about? Wasn't it only on Saturday that they met when I took him to lunch? And he did a drawing of me? What have I launched?"

Martin tried to be very quiet as he slipped out of bed, went to the bathroom. He poured a bowl of corn flakes with milk and dressed to meet Mr. James. As he approached the door, Ray raised up in bed and asked, "Where you goin', friend?"

"The more interesting question is, where have you been, friend? I noted that at ten thirty you weren't under the covers yet. Seems like a long time just for a painting session!"

"Have you gotten so old, in such a short time, that you've

forgotten what happens to guys when they're with women who are totally beautiful, inside and out? Come on, Martin, use your memory! End of story! At least for the moment!"

Martin grabbed a light sweater and headed off to Supreme Food Products, Inc. He arrived before almost anyone else was there. The custodians had left the outer door to the administration offices open. He walked in and looked about the office. There on the wall was another picture of Grandmother James, taken as a snapshot but enlarged to remind all of how Supreme Foods got its start. He walked over to the picture and was studying it when Miss Franks, the office manager, entered.

"Good morning, Mr. Roberts. Welcome to Supreme Foods."

"Good morning, Miss Franks. Isn't it amazing I remembered your name? I trust there's some things improving in the life of this voyager," Martin countered. "I guess I'm more than a little excited about coming back to Supreme Foods. I couldn't sleep, so I got up, dressed, and, because it was early, made the whole way here without one red traffic light. If I had been late all the lights would have been red. Murphy's Law, isn't it?"

Betsy Franks smiled at him. "It's good to see you looking so well, Mr. Roberts. Mr. James should be here soon. Meanwhile, here are some promotional materials to look at. I'll wager that much, if not all the material, is familiar. You probably helped to write it. If you'll excuse me I'll get things organized for Mr. James and his staff." Miss Franks gave herself fully to check phone messages, getting some correspondence written for Mr. James to sign, and much more that is done as a regular procedure.

The outer door to the administration suite suddenly opened and Mr. James rushed into the area.

"Good morning, Mitch. I'm sorry! Good morning, Martin. It's so good to see you here with us."

"I was studying the picture of your grandmother. Do you have any other snapshots of her? I don't know why that seems so important at the moment, but for some reason I'd like to think I really knew her. Her pictures and the stories of her life add understanding of her as a person. Who knows how that sometime it will come in handy," Martin confided.

"I'm sure we can get more pictures of her. But our big job today is to introduce or reintroduce you to each of the departments in the company. It's important that you get to know the people who work here for the company. It's equally important that the employees get to really know you. Let's give them some time to get settled in. I think it's important for you to see how everything works together. Come on in to my office and relax until we're ready to do the rounds. If you'll excuse me, I'll attend to some things that need my attention."

Mr. James read and signed papers and wrote some reminders of all he wanted to cover with Martin during the visit. Martin looked about the room making careful note of as many details as he could identify. At last Mr. James seemed satisfied, stacked the papers and got up from his desk.

"Come on, Martin. Let's get acquainted with the employees of Supreme Food Products" Together they visited those doing the packaging of the products in the bakery department, the department personnel that did the freezing of foods, and the shipping people. Not a single group was left out.

Martin thought for moment, then asked, "Where do all these people eat?"

"They either bring their own lunch or go out."

"Would it have any purpose if we were to establish a dining facility here in the complex where people could taste and test the products they're working with? We might call it 'FIRST LINE' meaning First Line of Approval. It may even provide employees an opportunity to make suggestions of how to support the company."

"Just how would we manage such a program?"

"I was so impressed with the work of the students from Lily Wong's Cooking School at the breakfast in which they prepared omelets. The quality of their work was superb. I noticed they were using Supreme Food Products materials. What would happen if graduates from Lily's school were to run such a restaurant and we opened it not only to our employees but also for interested community people who might not yet know of the quality of the foods the company supports?"

"Great idea, Martin! Let's talk it over with Leland and get his thoughts. If what I'm hearing from you is the importance of getting everyone in the company to take ownership in our work then we need to start with ourselves."

"I've heard that Leland was very interested in developing use of Supreme Foods, and that in the report of the City Council's lunch prepared by the students, Leland had a big hand in helping the students. A part of marketing might be the creating of recipes using the company products in some new and interesting combinations. I understand that is the strong emphasis of Lily's school. Such material would be a good 'sell' potential. Who knows, the marketing might result in the publication of a cook book, the spreading knowledge of Lily Wong's Cooking School and the demand for our products."

"You're amazing! These ideas have great potential. I must invite Leland to join us for more discussion on the topic. Have you seen your office yet? We had workers here over the weekend getting your space ready. Let's go take a look!" Mr. James led the way down the hall to the room next door. He opened the door and invited Martin to the room."

"Good grief! The space is almost as big as my apartment. It looks wonderful. The only thing missing is a park across the street, a blind with a slit to let the light from the street lights in," and, after a pause, "a Dr. Bonner to bring sunshine in on a dreary day."

"I've observed that you're turned on by Beatrice! "

"She has helped me out of my shell. I lost a son in a traffic accident. I divorced Gladys, my wife, and when I applied for the presidency of Supreme Foods and you chose your son I was devastated. I wanted to hide. I even took a simple one-room apartment where I thought no one would find me. Thanks to a cloud burst and the need to help Dr. Bonner to her office, I was imprisoned in her office. She kept inviting me out of myself. I learned I could not hide. Then I heard your voice at the breakfast. I froze, not wanting to face you. You came rushing over, turned me around and with the warmest handshake greeted me and told me two things: Randall Garrett wanted to see me about A and P selling our products, and you asked would I return to the company. I had to excuse myself. I didn't want anyone to see a grown man cry. I met with you and Leland. You said the decision to return must be my own decision. So this morning I could not sleep. I awakened very early. I felt like a young man about to go on his first date, excited about the possibilities but wanting to make sure I met everyone's expectation. I still don't know how all of this will turn out, but I'm beginning to trust myself in what I give myself to."

"Wow! What an amazing story, Martin. But isn't that true for each one of us? We don't know for sure what lies ahead for us. We can't change history. We can learn from it and we don't know what tomorrow will bring. If we are true to the moment and give it our best, we'll be ready to take on tomorrow. I'm very pleased you are willing to share with us. By the way, everyone calls me Jimmy. I guess my parents got stuck on the name James, and "James James" doesn't work too well."

"Thank you, Jimmy. Sounds strange, but I'll get used to it!"

With that, Jimmy James, shook Martin's hand, faced the door, and left the room.

Standing alone in his new office, Martin pinched himself to see if he were alive or just having a wonderful dream. "How can so much happen in such a short time? Was it only five days ago that I was awakened by a cloudburst and a young lady needing to be saved from a heavy rain?" he thought to himself. He looked on the wall opposite the book shelves, not yet containing a book, to see a picture of Grandmother James, reminding him of what the company stood for.

Martin packed some tablets in his brief case and headed for the door. Miss Franks spoke to him as he passed her desk.

"A Mr. Randall Garrett called while you were being shown around the various departments. He is planning to be in Bloomfield next week on Thursday and would like to pick up on some conversation you had with him a few weeks ago. He also said he would challenge you to a game of golf."

"That is a challenge! He wins every time. I wondered what he does beside golf?" Martin said with, a note of playfulness in his voice. "Tell him I'll wipe the rust from my clubs and be ready to take him on!" With a smile on his face he disappeared from his new space.

Chapter 14

Getting the Ball Rolling

Martin wanted very much to share with Ray the events of the day. He rushed back to his apartment, hurriedly parked his car, and almost ran up the stairs. He flung open the door to explode into the room.

"Well, Mr. Artist, what have we here? The twentieth century Mona Lisa? Impressive! Who is she?"

"Mr. Roberts, your mind is failing you. Have you no memory? It's my new friend, the waitress at the restaurant, surely you remember her?"

"But I don't remember her as being that beautiful!" Martin added.

"That's because you're not an artist. The power of the painting of Mona Lisa is that the artist invited us to look more deeply into the character being painted. Learning to see, hear and feel the depth of an expression is what I'm attempting to share."

"Thank you, professor. But then, there is an element of that in what I try to do in marketing products." Martin sat on the side of his bed and began thinking.

"Grandmother James! Grandmother James! Ray Wynn! Ray Wynn! Why do these names keep popping up in my mind? What's the connection?" he questioned himself. "I think I need to go back to the Packaging Department. Perhaps that's where I'll find an answer. Why is Grandmother James' picture in my office?"

Martin watched Ray add little touches to his painting, small touches that suddenly gave new depth to his work. He thought to himself, "I think an answer is taking shape in my feeble brain. I must revisit the packaging department at Supreme Foods. I'll have Ray come with me to view the pictures of Grandmother James. Something is beginning to happen," he reasoned.

"Ray, I want you to see my new office. It's as large almost, as this apartment. But it doesn't have a park across the street or a Beatrice Bonner to visit... well, at least not yet!" Martin did not reveal the real intent, that of seeing the pictures of Grandmother James. To himself, he thought, "I'll spring that on him when he sees the pictures. Perhaps he'll see something of the soul of Supreme Products!"

The following day, with Ray in his company, he went to Supreme Food Products. They went directly to the packaging department. To one of the employees he asked, "Tell me your name again. I heard so many names when I was introduced that I can't get names and faces together."

"Paul Wright. That doesn't mean I'm always right!" he said with a chuckle.

"Paul, this is my friend Ray Wynn. I think he's a Wynner! Ray, meet Paul Wright!" Martin added.

"Paul, show me one of the packages you ship out from the company."

Paul brought a large package ready for delivery. "We try to keep the language legible and strong."

"What does the package say to you about Supreme Food Products?"

"I'm not sure what you're asking. We try to be straightforward and easy to read."

"What do you hear Mr. James say about the products created here? Is there certain language which spells out what he wants customers to remember?"

"I'll have to give that special thought. Thanks for asking the question." With that he handed Martin a package that was ready for shipment.

"Thanks, Paul. This is going to be very helpful." He left carrying his new prize with him. "Now, to get Ray thinking about the problem. He is so perceptive. He'll have an answer!" He set the package on a table beneath the picture of Grandmother James. "The problem is becoming clearer. I may have an answer. I'll talk it over with Ray,"

Changing the subject, Martin, thinking aloud said, "I wonder what gourmet treat is in store tonight. If I want toast I'd better stop for bread! But cornflakes again? I don't think so!"

Ray did observe that Martin had placed the package beneath the picture of the elderly woman.

Ray was thinking to himself, "Now what is this all about? Is it like the tablet and pens when we went to the little restaurant? Martin has a way of setting the stage for what he hopes will happen." He centered his attention on the picture above the package. "When will I hear what is expected of me?" He turned to see Martin putting some things together to leave his office. They returned to the apartment, Ray to his painting and Martin, slipping down the stairs and across the street to the park with high hopes that Beatrice would be there.

Chapter 15

Beginning First Line

Martin was excited about going to work. The echo of Ray's description of finding the soul within his painting still sounded in Martin's mind. "Oh, to find the soul of Supreme Foods," he thought. "What will the magic of this day be?" He grabbed a light jacket, slipped it on, and raced down the stairs to go to his car. He eagerly drove his car to the parking lot at Supreme Foods.

The first person he saw was Paul from the shipping department. "Good morning, Paul. You're getting here early. Have a great day!" as he extended his hand in friendship and greeting.

Paul broke into a big smile and thought, "What is this man about? I seldom have such warm greetings. Is this part of a new trend? Whatever it is, I like it!" He struck up a tune whistling as he bounded to the Shipping Department.

Martin went directly to his office, but no other soul had yet gotten to work. He sat briefly at his desk, but then got up and went to study Grandmother James' picture. His memory flashed back to the interview he had with Mr. James when applying for the presidency position. He thought, "I wanted to increase the profit as a way of making Supreme Food more competitive. Mr. James reminded me that it was the quality of Grandmother James' cooking that started the company. Quality will be the company's standard." He stood for a moment then, smashing his fist into the other hand said aloud, "That's it. 'Quality is the standard'. I think I know now why the names of Grandmother James and Ray Wynn were bouncing around in my brain!"

As he was about to cut a caper, as if on a dance floor, the door opened to see Jimmy James and his son Leland standing there smiling at the exhibition of excitement. "Well, Mr. Roberts, in what show are you planning to enlist in? What's playing on Broadway that could use such a dance? Would it be alright if the president of Supreme Foods and I had a conversation with you? I've shared a bit of your idea with Leland but I'd like you to share more of what you're thinking."

Martin pulled up a chair in front of his desk and faced Leland and Jimmy. He began, "I hardly know where to begin. So much is racing through my brain. Oh yes, the idea of the First Line of Approval, a lunch room for the employees to get together, to learn to know each other, and to become more fully engaged in Supreme Foods." He paused to collect his thoughts.

Leland spoke, "I like the idea of our employees becoming more engaged in the work of the company. How would a lunch room help with that?"

Martin continued, "I was so impressed with the breakfast prepared at the church by students from Lily Wong's Cooking School. I'm also aware of the number of products that have come from Lily's Cooking School and have become standards in our offerings. What if every item considered were to be approved by groups before being presented to the general public? The employees, with a personal interest in the work of the company, would sample the foods and become the First Line of Approval. And as Lily or any of the cooking staff create new recipes from our products those products become our growing product line. We might work out a system when major products are created and accepted, the person, or persons, might be awarded shares in the company. Then, not only would they be interested in what they had created but now they would have a vested interest in the company. My hunch is that they would work doubly hard to make everything succeed."

Jimmy rose from his chair and went to face the picture of Grandmother James. "What do you think, Grandma?" he asked aloud. "If we keep the quality up would it work?" There was a long pause, a time for thinking to happen. Finally Jimmy James turned to face Martin. "Martin, I like the idea. I want all our employees to feel they have an important interest in what we are doing. Where would such a dining area be set up?"

"That's something we could invite members of the staff to decide. We need to invite them to feel fully a part of the process. It might be set up so that people who are not employees could come and be a part of the process. I'm sure we'd want to make sure that the quality is there before presenting it to the general public." He paused again, and then continued. "We might invite the employees to make suggestions of how the food would be presented. For example, my Aunt Grace's Hickory Nut Cake has been a favorite in our family for years. It might be a dessert for a few days, with people deciding whether it should be sold as a fully baked and packaged product, to be done as a mix with people adding an egg and milk, or in some other form. We'd prepare a response sheet to be completed after eating the cake."

"Leland jumped right in with, "I like that idea. Ever since I met with Lily Wong and her students I've been intrigued with how we create new tastes by combining our products in fresh new ways. I'd wager that if we began such a process that people would want to know more ways of combining foods to achieve new tastes. A cook book would be in the making. We might even call it Grandma James' Cook Book and emphasize the quality of foods from Supreme Food Products."

"You're getting the spirit. Who knows where all this will take us if we pool our ideas?" Martin replied. Jimmy nodded and smiled, pleased with the progress being taken.

"We'll look the building over and see where a lunchroom might fit our purposes best," Jimmy added. "What more do you have, Martin?"

"A couple more ideas are taking shape, but I have to think them through more clearly, maybe even getting something down on paper."

Father and son looked at each other and without saying a word, conveyed their approval to each other. "We have work to do, so we'll have to run. Thanks, Martin, for your suggestions. We'll talk it over and probably get most of it in action." With that they both excused themselves and returned to their offices.

Martin glanced at the picture of Grandmother James on the wall, "Well, good friend, I think we have something started. Don't ever let me forget your standard for quality!" As the two men left, Miss Franks came to door and reminded Martin, "Tomorrow is Thursday. Remember to dust off the rust from your golf clubs. Be ready to take Mr. Garrett on. I think he's aching for a challenge. I somehow think it might happen tomorrow. Also, a Ray Wynn called to say he's ready for that job you want him to do but that you keep up the suspense by not telling him what it is. How does he know about Grandmother James?" She thought for a moment then added, "The game going on here is beyond my thinking. I look forward to meeting Ray Wynn. He sounds like a playful sort of a guy!" She closed the door and returned to her desk and the work before her.

Martin packed his briefcase with work to be thought through when he got back to the apartment. He was eager to share with Ray what had taken place with Leland and Jimmy James. As he bounded up the stairs and flung open the door, there stood Ray wearing a painter's smock, with a cap tilted on his head and paint brushes held between his teeth.

"Oh, Sir Roberts, Sir. You are looking at a painter, filled with satisfaction for having completed the masterpiece of his life – a painting of the glamorous, seductive woman in my life. Can I help it if seduction is only in my thoughts? Well, at least I can look at her picture and use my imagination.

"I can tell by the way you ripped through the door that you're in no mood just to listen to my raving about a beautiful woman. But then, what more is there?"

"So much has happened today. So much has happened since that Wednesday cloudburst! And I can tell by the way you're standing with paint brushes in your mouth that you're in no mood to listen to my raving about a day at Supreme Foods! Perhaps you might be interested in an illustrating job?"

"For money? You mean a job using my art that is connected to money?"

"Exactly! I'm sure you saw the package ready for shipment that I set directly under the picture of Grandmother James? Supreme Foods have an unspoken rule that their products must have quality, that it was the quality of Grandma James' foods that started the company, and it's the quality that they want to be known for. Would it be possible for you to draw a picture of the grandmother and add the words 'A Grandma James Quality Product'? We're opening a lunch room at the company so employees and friends of the company can play a part in the First Line of Approval of products. It would be good if one of the very first choices would be to decide the most appropriate design to be placed on each product being shipped from the company. Having watched you drawing, I'd like to invite you to prepare some options that the employees would approve of for our use. Interested?"

"Interested? Does water run down hill? Is the Pope Catholic? Do I like to eat?" Ray paused then added, "I guess I could try. It's what I did most of my life. When do I get started? Do you have more pictures of Grandmother James?"

"I've asked the family to share more pictures of their grandmother, a great grandmother for some of them. I'll bring them to you just as soon as they bring them in. Perhaps you might go in with me tomorrow. Oh no, not tomorrow. Tomorrow I have Randall Garrett from the A & P Company coming to see me. He wants to try a game of golf starting early tomorrow morning. How about Friday? I'd like you to get to know the people in some of the departments."

"Done deal! Friday it'll be," With that, the paint brushes went back between his teeth as he stood to admire the completed painting. "Wow, what a woman!"

Chapter 16

The Game is Golf-Thursday

The street light had gone off. The hint of sunshine and the light of early dawn silhouetted the buildings to the east. Ray had bounced out of bed eager to begin his day. He quickly finished his bathroom routines then returned to raise the blinds to let in daylight.

With a loud voice he began, "Hey, you snoring wonder, are you part bear beginning an early hibernation? I thought you had an early golf game. Are you planning to sleep through your game of golf? Up and at 'em!"

Martin raised himself up in bed, shook his head, and threw back the covers. Martin had over slept. He glanced at the one clock the room supported.

"Good grief! I've done it again. If I'm not careful I'll be late for my meeting with Randall Garrett. Randall is the chief buyer for the A & P Company," he muttered to himself as he jerked himself out of bed. He rushed to the bathroom and swiped his razor across his face. "Oh damn. Cut myself. Must I have such a terrible beginning of the day? No time for breakfast! Oh nuts. I hate myself for being such a loser!" He was surprised that the old feelings had returned.

Martin slipped into a clean shirt and his casual pants as he brushed his hair and began his race from the room. Getting a few step down the stairs, "Oh, damn. I forgot my bag and the clubs!"

He raced back up, grabbed his bag and clubs and descended down the stair to his car. Throwing the bag in his car trunk, he jumped into his seat, started the motor and tore out of the parking garage and headed toward the Supreme Food Products offices.

Martin raced to the outer office. "Miss Franks, I've an appointment with Randall Garrett that I don't want to appear to be late for. Cover for me, if you will. I want to really impress him. He is important to our company."

Miss Franks tried to silence Martin by putting her fingers to her lips as she tilted her head to the seats in the outer office. There sat Randall Garrett. Martin, blushing as he faced Randal, said, "Well, oversleeping and not having time for breakfast, is no assurance that one doesn't end up with egg on his face!

"Well, how is this for a start? Just when I wanted to impress you! Let me get a couple of things from my desk and we'll be off," Martin said.

"If you haven't had anything to eat, perhaps our first stop should be at a place where there's food. I could use a cup of coffee," Randall said. "You need to keep your strength up, especially if we're going to do eighteen holes!"

"Somehow I feel like I'm going to give you a run for your money! We'll give it a try! Do we have time to engage the new Marley Hotel? Some of the graduates of Lily Wong's Cooking School manage the restaurant. We hear the food is excellent. The treat is on me." Martin charged to his office and picked up some papers he had prepared the day before.

"I'll drive. There are some things I want to make sure you know about, things I think may change patterns of marketing. Right now we need to head out to the Country Club. Get your bag and clubs. I'll get my car and meet you in the parking lot." Martin said his good-byes to Miss Franks. "Tell Mr. James and Leland that I'll see them later this afternoon. I'm sorry to miss their meeting with chairs of department as they talk about the proposed diner." With that he was gone.

Martin drove his car to the public parking lot and stopped behind Randall's car. They threw Randall's bag and clubs into Martin's trunk. They jumped into the car and were off to the Marley Hotel.

"It seems to me that a lot of building is going on in Bloomfield, or is it at the outskirts of the city? Looking at where building is happening is something we must be aware of." Randall stated.

"That's part of what I want to discuss with you following the game," Martin offered. "But I want you to see what is taking place and how that impacts our work. Right now my stomach tells me it's time to chew on something other than an idea."

Little was said as they pulled into the parking lot at the Marley. They jumped out of the car and headed for the restaurant. They were met by a host.

"May we help you?" the host asked.

"I want a breakfast that's gonna help me beat my friend here on the golf course. He has a tradition of always beating me. It's time to disrupt traditions!" Martin replied.

"The usual is good enough for me. I'll just do with a cup of coffee," Randall quipped.

"I'm sure our staff will give you exactly what you want. We aim to please!" the host exclaimed, trying to be diplomatic. He took them to a window seat which looked out over the golf course. "Perhaps seeing the course and thinking about your game may help you achieve what you want." He placed the menus in front of them and opened the napkins to find their resting places on their laps. "Enjoy your breakfast!"

The two men glanced at the menu. "I wonder if Supreme Food Products helps to guarantee satisfaction?" Randall asks.

"Who knows? Lily Wong's a strong supporter of Supreme products," Martin offered.

"The A & P Company is aware of the increase in the number of children and the potential for new products to serve this population. Did I remember hearing you say something about a product called 'Baby Supreme' or was I just dreaming?" Randall asked. "It's a large new market, especially if the baby food is especially focused on health. Parents are becoming more conscious of quality foods.

I have often heard your company talk about quality products. Was that not the basis of the company being formed?"

"Absolutely!" Martin replied. "I have many things to share with you of how we plan to assure that quality remains the core of our work. That's the topic for the third hole!

The waiter came to the table. "May I have you order, please? Our special today is the Marley's Supreme omelet- three cheeses, bacon, artichokes, onion and peanuts!"

"Peanuts? Who ever heard of peanuts in an omelet? Randall asked.

"Part of our exploration at Supreme Foods is to try new combinations of products we produce and market. Students from Lily Wong's Cooking School prepared a breakfast for the people of the neighborhood. They prepared omelets for everyone. We each could choose what we wanted in our omelet. Not wanting to make choices I simply said 'Everything'. They put peanuts in my omelet. I had never had peanuts in an omelet before. I was surprised at how good the omelet was and the pleasure the texture added to the taste. You must try it sometime," Martin explained.

"Great. Tell the chef to create an omelet for me with his most creative imagination. Be sure to add peanuts," Randall said in his request.

"I'll make it simple, do the same for me!" Martin added.

It seemed like no time had passed when the waiter returned with their sumptuous treats.

"Looks like I'll be doing more than coffee!" Randall said smiling his satisfaction for the beauty of the presentation. "Probably not much lunch for me today!"

The conversation never seemed to stray far from the food they were served. As they finished the last bite and put away the last drop of coffee, Randall motioned for the waiter to come to their table. "Tell the chef he can make omelets for me anytime I am in Bloomfield. It was excellent. From now on all my omelets will have peanuts. I'll bet that will raise some eyebrows!"

Martin and Randall wiped their mouths and smacked their lips.

Martin paid the bill as Randall left a generous tip.

"That was one of your best ideas ever, Marty," Randall added as they made their way to their car and the golf course.

They checked in at the golf course. The attendant observed, "No offense, Mr. Roberts, but you are a little past the time you requested. It's lucky Thursdays aren't heavy days on our course."

"Sorry about that," Martin added. "I must confess that I overslept, didn't have breakfast, so Mr. Garrett thought I needed sustenance if we were going to do eighteen holes. We ordered breakfast with my requesting food adequate to beat Mr. Garrett. He said 'the usual' is good enough for me, meaning, I think, he intends to beat me again. Well, it's time to break traditions. Wish me luck."

"We show no favoritism. We wish every person a best game," the attendant answered.

As they began their first strokes, Randall led off placing his tee on the ground, the ball on the tee, then, drawing back, swung his club with a mighty stroke. They watched the ball's flight to the flag on the first hole.

"Wow! You're incredible, Randall. You landed on the green. Now, my turn!" Martin set his tee, mounted the ball and prepared for the drive. In one magnificent swing drove the ball on its way.

"Okay, how'd you do it? Did you see that? A hole in one! Have you given up selling so you could spend more time at the golf course?" Randall said, almost in disbelief.

"Beginner's luck! It never happened before in my lifetime. I usually have to go find my ball somewhere in the rough. However, it does feel good!" Martin asserted.

The game progressed as one might expect. "Did we say we'd deal with the subject of baby food at the second or the third hole? What is it that A & P wants produced in the field of baby foods?" Martin asked.

"I need to share with you what I see happening in the marketing field," Randall began. "We seem to be moving away from private labels in the industry. A & P Company began marketing private label products in the late 1800's with modified names for the products.

We set the stage for what is becoming a more common practice."

"Interesting," Martin exclaimed. "I never realized the part your company has played in the food business. What else is shaping such decisions?"

Randall picked up the conversation."The whole advertising approach has begun to change. I'm sure that you really look at how radio and television have begun to reshape selling. Consumers are becoming increasingly aware of the quality of food and the prices. Companies like Gerber's are already exploring the special market for babies. Such companies tend to be conservative but are beginning to fortify their products with vitamins and minerals. Baby foods are being packaged in containers easy to warm before feeding. I would think finding new ways of packaging of some foods coming in dry form that are easy to perhaps add warm milk or water prior to feeding would be helpful. Parents could then prepare only as much food as needed so there is an economy factor, also. 'Baby Supreme' could be the first to feature organic, and health food for the coming generation of parents that will become the trend setters."

The playing golf had virtually stopped, so interested were they in brainstorming a possible food product. From behind them, "Hey, you guys. Are you here to play golf, or just have a friendly chat?"

"Sorry," Martin said to the young man and woman behind them. "We're talking about the best food that we can create for healthy babies. Some things seem to take preference in our lives."

"Baby food? Now that's something we often talk about! Our year old child requires we find the best baby food at the grocery," the man replied. "May we join you? Sounds like something we'd be interested in."

"Come by the new First Line Cafe at Supreme Food Products Company and we'll share what we're creating. You might even be one of our couples that would advise us on the quality of our Baby Supreme line of foods for the very young," Martin added. "Here let me give you my card. I'd also like you to meet Mr. Randall Garrett of the A & P Company. I'm sure you know much about what his company does to provide the finest in food quality and value. Why don't the two of you play on through? Mr. Garrett traditionally beats me in the game of golf. Today I'm trying to break traditions. Perhaps we can do that on this course and in our industry."

The time seemed to fly, so involved were they in thinking through details of their businesses. As they had finished the eighteenth hole they each added their score.

Alright, Martin, what's your total?" Randall asked. "I have 72."

"Ah hah! I did it! I won, but only by one point. I hope we both won with the conversation we had while playing. I know I have a new field to explore," Martin replied. "Here we are without a product as yet. Now Supreme Foods has the potential of working with the second largest company in the United States, second only to General Motors. I think the people working in Supreme Foods will 'puff up' at that thought. I'll bet we'll end up giving you exclusive rights to Baby Supreme foods for at least a year."

"If that happens, A & P will give special shelf space to your products for that same period." Randall exclaimed. "Martin, you're a man of vision. How lucky Supreme Foods is to have you in a driver's seat," Randall volunteered. "After all that thinking and walking the full course, even after my additional breakfast, I think I'm ready for lunch. Lunch is on A & P."

"I do want to show you something that I feel is significant. It is a building project on the main road between Baronsville and Bloomfield. It's not far out of our way to where we'll go for lunch." Martin suggested.

Little was said as they approached the main highway. There on the west side of the road, in what had previously been a large wheat field, were graders, trucks, cranes and workers beginning to create a structure of some size.

Martin began, "I am told this is to be the new Kroger Store. The store is larger than any other stores in the area. I hear they have a large storage area, space capable of holding quantities of food they expect to sell. Note the graded space before the building. I hear it'll be a parking lot. People can park right close to the door of the store, buy their groceries and be quickly on their way. What does that suggest about future marketing?"

"I must report this back to our headquarters. I do know they want to keep the friendly small service area option that has served them well in the past. The question is always about how do we meet the new developments while retaining the 'down home', friendly feeling previously established?" Randall replied.

"We don't know the answer to new directions being taken. Are we even sure of what the central questions really are? I do know we must keep abreast of trends being taken, otherwise we'd still be manufacturing buggy whips," Martin volunteered.

Each of the men was in deep thought as they drove on their way to Martin's favorite restaurant which he called the "hole in the wall" cafe.

When they arrived at the cafe and entered the dining area, they were met by the manager. "Great to see you, Martin. Did you see Ray busy at work at his 'studio' in the window of the restaurant? I'm amazed at his artistic ability. He's really giving this place a high quality in the minds of our customers. I'm pleased at how his work brings us customers who care about the quality of our food."

He had barely ended his expression of enthusiasm, when the waitress appeared. Randall looked at the woman and then gave his full attention to the painting hanging behind her.

"How can a beauty like you not be working in the most prestigious restaurant in Bloomfield? That painting is amazing. The artist bared your very soul. Seeing the painting makes me want to know that person even more. Has anyone compared this painting with the Mona Lisa? The painter has shown the beauty that is deep within." Randall exclaimed, being very moved by what he saw.

Martin motioned, "Ray, come here, I want you to meet a friend who understands your art."

Ray left his easel in the front window and came to the table where Randall and Martin sat, and the waitress stood waiting.

"Ray, I want you to meet Randall Garrett, the major buyer for the A & P Company. He's very impressed with your painting. He sees things, apparently, as an artist sees. Randall, this is Ray Wynn, someone I think will make some great contributions to Supreme Foods Company. We're lucky to have found him."

"Good to meet you, Mr. Garrett. And thank you for the affirmation of my work. I must confess that as I have worked on this painting I've become biased concerning the model. But then, isn't that what life is all about?" Ray asked.

"Would that all people could find that joy in their work! I've learned to appreciate the ability of others in their work. As is often stated, 'I have never made an apple pie but I know a good one when I taste it.' Perhaps that is what we are all called to do, to be able to affirm each other and affirm their best qualities," Randall added. "Expressing the best in others and caring about them would make our world a better place."

"Why are you a buyer when the world needs to hear what you've just expressed?" Ray asked.

"It is, when in each of our tasks we express such things, we begin to change the world in which we live. I don't need to be a great writer or philosopher to make a difference. It is the little things we do, day by day, that make the greatest difference," said Randall.

Martin sat fully engaged with the conversation but not saying a word. It was then he added, "Now I know why being on the golf course with you has been so important to me. I'm just beginning to discover that my greatest joy is in the empowerment of others!"

"I can say 'Amen' to that. I was almost a beggar when Martin found me and he invited me back to life. Now I must serve others with the gifts I possess. If I can do that I feel that I will have helped, in some small way, to make our world a better place to live. Isn't it interesting when that kind of thinking is happening, everything seems to turn out right?" Ray said. "Excuse me, I need to get back to my work and your gorgeous waitress wants to take your order. But then, I'm not prejudiced!" Smiling, as he moved back to the front window.

"I'm sorry, Dotty. This is Randall Garrett, a buyer from A & P Company who delights in always beating me at the game of golf. Today we broke that tradition. Randall, this Dorothy Denver, Ray's favorite model. I don't know what the next painting will be, but I'm sure it will involve Dotty," Martin quickly added.

Dotty said, "Good to meet you, Mr. Garrett. What may I get for you? Our special today is black bean chili and a half pound burger with Swiss cheese, bacon, onion and avocado."

"I doubt I'd starve with a meal like that. I'd like a glass of ice tea, too," Randall replied.

"Double the order," Martin said. "Everything here is good. And the service is superb. Thanks, Dotty."

Both men directed their attention to Ray's painting and the sketches of customers who asked Ray to draw their faces. The food was served almost too quickly and consumed. Randall paid the bill. Martin left a generous tip and they were gone.

Chapter 17

Baronsville Anew

As sunlight, coming later each day, broke the quietness of the room, Martin glanced up at the calendar. "September is history. What a month! So much! So intense! So awakening!" Crawling out of bed he moved to the calendar to change the dates to October with the picture of the autumn colors.

"Dr. Bonner, I mean Beatrice, loves going to the park to experience the beauty of nature," he thought to himself. "Perhaps I might take her out of the city to see October in its full glory." He thought for a moment. "I didn't take time to see and feel the beauty when I lived in Baronsville. I did hear people talk about it. I think I'll call her and drive her down to the area around Baronsville. 'Tis true, they've begun to build houses for bedroom communities in the area, in fact on a part of the farm that we once owned."

Martin lay in bed awaiting Ray's awakening from a deep sleep. "More painting sessions late at night?" he playfully entertained the thought. "He and that waitress seem to be having more and longer painting sessions!"

It was six thirty when Ray stretched his body under the covers and gurgled the sounds of awakening. "What time is it?" he asked. "That was quite a late session. I wonder how other painters worked when painting nudes?"

"Do you mean to have me believe that the motivation was purely artistic?" Martin countered. "Somehow I'm not fully convinced. But I am willing to study the final work."

"Don't try to discredit me, you dirty old man! You'll be moved by the elegance of that body!"

"I don't have time to say more about whatever this is about. I'm taking my psychologist to see the beauty of autumn. I think, if she is available, we'll go down to the area around Baronsville to see the colors and the sensuousness of October."

Ray smiled. "Do you mean to have me believe that this is purely for the purpose of exploring nature? The nature of what? You may be middle aged, man, but you're not dead!"

"Go back to sleep while I call Beatrice," Martin added

"Now the secret is out. It's no longer Dr. Bonner but now Beatrice! You gotta watch your language, man, lest you betray your motivation." Ray turned over pretending to go back to sleep.

Martin picked up the phone and called Beatrice. She answered. Martin, with an edge of excitement, began. "If you're available, I thought we might take a drive down to the area around Baronsville. It will be in full sunlight. They tell me the colors are spectacular and everything about the season is a feast for the senses."

Ray smiled and thought, "Now he's revealing himself. Sensuous? What purpose sensuousness?"

Beatrice quickly responded. "That sounds like what the good doctor ordered, at least this doctor. I'll have to change a couple of appointments, which I can do, or have the secretary do. I can be ready by about eight o'clock.'

"I'll pick you up at your apartment. Dress casually for we'll be exploring nature."

"Okay, friend, there are some things you can't hide. You've gotta be ready with a full report after this exploration!" Ray bounded out of bed and headed for the shower. Playfully he began singing with a rich, full voice, "Eency, weency, spider."

Martin put his hands over his ears as he grabbed his coat and his car keys. "I'm going out for a bite of breakfast. You're on your own, if you're responsible enough!" he added teasingly. He thought, "Just time to feed the face and be ready for a most wonderful day!"

In no time he was at his favorite restaurant. As he finished his last bite he looked at his watch. "Oh nuts, it's already seven thirty. I can't be late this morning, too. I have no way of knowing what will happen but the promises are high." He finished his breakfast quickly then rushed to his car and sped on to Beatrice's apartment building. As he pulled up in front he saw her waiting for him. "Hmmm. Is she as excited about this adventure as I? Couldn't be!"

Martin jumped out of his car, got behind Beatrice, pushing her wheelchair to the front side passenger seat. Using her crutches, she raised herself and moved to the seat. Martin collapsed her chair and placed it in the trunk of his car. He closed the trunk, then raced to the driver's seat, demonstrating his excitement for what he anticipated for them.

"We'll drive toward Baronsville, passing through the farms the James owns, and where they began the cooking by Grandmother James that became Supreme Foods. Many of the farms around Baronsville have been sold to make big money. Even the farm where we once lived for less than a year, we sold for a big profit. Some of the land is still as we found it. Other parts are becoming bedroom communities. But we'll explore as much of October beauty as we can find."

Beatrice nodded her approval and sat not wanting to disturb the quietness that began her day. After a short time she added, "Martin, this is very kind of you. You know how much I value the beauty of nature. I find such natural beauty awakens my very soul. You are giving me a very special gift. Thank you!" Nothing more needed to be added as they passed through the country, observing every detail along the way.

They passed through "downtown" Baronsville and on to the place where Martin, Gladys and Jack had lived. Martin pulled up in the driveway, a space he knew only too well. Behind them and to their right, the sounds of graders, trucks and other heavy equipment drowned out the beauty of a quiet morning and the awakening of nature. No longer could the sound of a bird's call and the echo from another be heard. The gentle sound of a morning breeze stirring the grass and the leaves of trees were gone. All that was dominant were the colorful trees on the hillside on the other side of the highway and beyond the barn. Without a word, they sat looking at the colors as rich as a painter's palette.

It was Beatrice who began the conversation. "Oh, I can almost hear the rustling of the grass and the sound of the birds. What a magnificent place this was. You were very lucky."

"It would have been good if I had been present. I was so centered in what I thought my life was about." Martin wanted to reach over and physically touch Beatrice. A couple of times he began to move his hand toward her but then withdrew it. Beatrice was fully aware of his struggle. She reached over putting her hand on his. Martin felt a surge of energy within him. He moved closer to share his feelings in a kiss.

As he bent over to kiss her, he glanced beyond her to the basketball backboard and hoop that Gladys had someone install to give their son a chance to practice his game. He lightly kissed Beatrice on her cheek.

"Is that all there is?" she asked.

"I'm sorry. For a moment I was very confused. I saw the basketball backboard and hoop and my mind was filled with what I hadn't done for my family. Forgive me."

"There's no need to be sorry. What you thought is often experienced. It is what we call in psychology as an anchor. The steeple and the cross on top of the church is an anchor. When people see it they are conditioned to enter the building in a special way. If you were entering a bar with brilliant neon signs advertising beers and you entered to noise, your entrance would be extremely different. What just happened is normal. Are there unfinished things that you must attend to?" Beatrice asked in response to his confession.

"When our son was killed in an automobile accident, I went home grieving on my own. Gladys had already moved into Jack's room. She must have been devastated by the event. I was not of any help to her in her time of pain. Why is it only now that this has stopped me from what I want so much and which is so important to me?"

"Is there something you feel you must do, something that was left unfinished?" Beatrice asked.

"I feel I must find Gladys to ask her forgiveness. Perhaps that will clear my memory. If I went to find her would you go with me?" Martin asked.

"That is probably something you must do alone. I do affirm your decision to do just that. I do not know where our relationship will go, and while that may be important now, there are other things that I suspect are even more important. Would you take me back to my apartment? This day I'll remember as long as I live. You've made a giant leap into your future." With that Martin started the car and they began their trip back to Bloomfield.

Little was said, but it was obvious that thinking was in high gear. When they arrived at Beatrice's apartment, Martin retrieved her chair, pushing it to the side of the car. Beatrice, using her crutches, lifted herself from her seat. She stood standing as if waiting for something to happen. Martin caught the clue. He carefully embraced her and kissed her fully. "I'm becoming more deeply in love with you. Heaven help me!"

"Now that's what a kiss should be!" she said smiling her satisfaction. She turned to seat herself in her chair. Martin pushed her through the apartment door and to the elevator. "Thank you, Martin. You are a blessing!" She pushed the UP button, awaited the elevator, and soon disappeared. Martin clapped his hands. "Life is so filled with blessings when one is open to them," he thought. He got back in his car and carefully, taking his time, drove back to his one-room apartment.

Chapter 18

Finding Gladys – Saturday

Friday night was a most disturbing one. All night long Martin tossed and turned, unable to sleep soundly. His thoughts were fully about the pending session with Gladys. Would she accept him? Has the pain of her losses subsided? What might she be giving herself to after their divorce? Would she have gone back to Pierce, Ohio, where they had first met as teenagers? Does she still feel betrayed when, while exploring our relationship, she became pregnant? Has she kept the Roberts name? How can I find her? Must I go? What if she rejects me and my needs to be forgiven?

It was nearly 2:30 in the morning when Martin fell asleep. He was awakened by the sound of Ray taking his shower. Drying himself, Ray donned his shorts and emerged. "What's in store for the great one today?" he asked. "Does Saturday spell something special?"

Martin pushed back the covers on his bed. They reflected the turmoil of the night, bunched in a pile at the foot of his bed. Martin rubbed his eyes attempting to get awake. "Last night is one that I'd prefer to never have again. Why can't the problems in life be resolved quickly and easily? Today I'm going to try to find my former wife and ask for her forgiveness for my not being present to our family's life. In that other life I lived, I thought I knew what was best for us. I thought achieving the presidency of Supreme Foods was what life was all about. In a sense I deserted my family. I'm going back to Pierce, Ohio, where we first met, hoping to find her and set things right. Part of me demands I do it. There is a part of me that fears rejection and wants to avoid the encounter. I was awake most of last night carrying on the conflict between those two parts of myself. Even now the internal dialog goes on."

"Well, friend, trust what you're setting out to do. Remember, it is the caring that helps to heal the pain in our lives. What you have shared about Gladys is that she is a caring person. Trust that!" Ray added.

"What sumptuous breakfast do we have to get the day started?" Martin asked.

"You'll be amazed at our choices: corn flakes from the box which you can have with milk or without. And we do have bread to make toast," Ray said in a playful mode.

Martin got out of bed, did his morning bathroom rituals and sat down to cornflakes with milk.

"You offer such wonderful options, Ray. Such imagination for our digestive track! I hope this lasts me through the morning."

Martin dressed with his best suit, white shirt and tie. "I must make a good impression," he thought. With a picture of Gladys and his son, Jack, Martin quietly slipped to the garage, got into his car and began his trip to Pierce. Twice he stopped at restaurants, he said for something to drink, but probably more for being unsure of how to begin the session with Gladys.

When he finally arrived in Pierce, he considered where the best place to inquire about Gladys would be. He decided that perhaps the drug store would have the best possibilities. He parked in front of the Leed's drug store, which hadn't changed much in the years since they were teenagers.

Going in, he approached the druggist. "I have a strange request. I'm looking for a woman that I once knew. Her name was Gladys Smith. She married a man by the name of Roberts. I'm unsure whether she still goes by the name of Roberts or if she took back her maiden name of Smith."

"Oh, yes. Everyone in Pierce knows Gladys Smith. She has become a real force in our community's library service. It's late in the day but my guess is that you'll find her at the library. She's dedicated to teaching children and helping them want to learn. You'll find the library," the druggist continued, with Martin interrupting,

"I do remember where the library is. Seems I remember how much Gladys enjoyed her time with books." Thank you, sir. You've been very helpful. I seem to remember you. How long have you been the druggist here in Pierce?" Martin asked.

"My whole life. The people of our village have become like a family. We care for each other. I can't imagine living anywhere else."

Martin quickly made his way to the library, asking the main librarian, "Where might I find Gladys Smith?"

"She's down the hallway and the second door on your right. It's the children's section, which Gladys has developed into a model program. Librarians from other towns come to consult with her about their library services for children. You'll be amazed by how she's organized her space. Thank you for being interested in the Pierce Library program," the librarian said.

Martin made his way down the hall to the second door on his right. He entered quietly. Gladys looked up and saw him, but quickly returned to reading a part of the story. Martin remembered many of the details of E. B. White's *Charlotte's Web*. There was comfort in hearing those familiar lines again.

Gladys stopped her reading at the point when Fern and her father take Wilbur to Uncle Homer Zuckerman's farm. "Now, friends, who would like to be Wilbur? And Fern? Fern's dad? Charlotte? Some of the other animals in the barn? Does Mr. White tell us anything about the time of day? What do you think Wilbur is feeling, being left alone in a strange place?" The children eagerly discussed the answers to her questions, volunteering to play various parts and talking about how it felt being alone when it's dark.

Parts were assigned to individual children. They began to dramatize that part of the story. They created dialog for each of the characters. "If Wilbur is so frightened, what might the animals do to help him be more comfortable?" Gladys asked.

"They could sing him a song to help him go to sleep," one replied.

"What do you call a song that helps someone sleep?" Gladys asked.

`After a short pause one child said, "A lullaby?"

"You're right, Bobby."

Gladys continued with the story. They talked about if it were dark, they'd tell him he'd see them in the morning and that Fern might come to see him after school. The drama began with every child involved and excited about what they were creating. At the end of the period, Gladys said, "Tomorrow we'll go on with the story. What do you think might happen to Wilbur? I wonder how the others will help him?" Each child stood up and went to Gladys for their hugs. It was a wonder to behold.

`When every child had departed, Gladys folded up her book, rearranged the chairs and the stage area in one corner of the room. She then went to Martin putting out her hand in greeting. "Well, Martin, what brings you to Pierce?"

"I'm trying to get my life back in order. I have found that there are things that I must deal with you. So much in our lives was never really cared for. I'd like to take you out to dinner so we can talk," Martin offered.

"I'm sorry. Pierce doesn't have any elegant restaurants. Anyway Franklin Pierce is coming to my house for dinner. Why don't you join us?" Gladys suggested. "I just got a new crock pot and I made a stew for dinner."

"I do remember your stews. What a special treat that will be!" Martin replied. "Who is this Franklin Pierce?"

"You'll get to know him over dinner. Will what you have to talk about be a problem if Franklin is with us?"

"Not for a minute. What I have to do is not easy. I must do it. Maybe he can be of help." Martin continued. "Where do you live?

Should I follow you to your house?

"Yes, follow me. Nothing is far away here in Pierce. You may remember Baronsville? Pierce is even smaller than Baronsville. Everyone knows everyone and everything about each other. Even with all of that we manage to accept and care for each other. Trust is high here in Pierce. I'll get my things I want to work on tonight. Librarians are teachers with many hours work to be done when students are not present. Give me about five to ten minutes and we'll be on our way." In no time they were leaving the library. It was only a short distance to her home. A new model Ford was parked in front of her house. They parked their cars and began their walk to the front door. Gladys said, "Looks like Franklin is here. I hope he has the table set. It will be no problem to add another place." They entered her house.

There were familiar pieces of furniture about the rooms. The red fire truck which they gave Jack on his third birthday held a place of prominence on the mantel. Jack's basketball trophies were encased in a glass fronted piece of furniture. Seeing these artifacts was most sobering. "Has she ever stopped grieving after Jack's death?" The need for what he must do became more evident.

"Martin, this is my friend Franklin Pierce. Franklin, this is my former husband Martin Roberts," Gladys said as she added another place setting at the table and set filled water glasses behind each plate.

"Franklin Pierce? Does that name have anything to do with the name of this village?" Martin asked.

"My great, great, grandfather, Tobias Pierce, moved here from Pennsylvania shortly after the Revolutionary War. He homesteaded a whole section of land. They were farmers and the land held promise. My great, great grandmother had eighteen children before Tobias died. Such families were needed in those days because so much had to be done by hand. Each of their children had big families until the area became known as Pierce's Place. Later the word 'Place' was dropped and the area became Pierce. With the advent of their families there developed a need for services. My great-grandfather

Pierce started a store. In his store they added a post office 'cause everyone came to the store for groceries and then they'd pick up their mail. There was little mail in those days," Franklin added.

"Franklin is the chair of our library board of directors. We work closely together," Gladys continued their history. "Then a little over a year ago his wife died, leaving him with four children, one out of high school and three still in school. At first I was lending a helping hand with problems he faced as a single parent. Our friendship has increased. He has asked me to move in with him. I have refused, for his children are not yet through the grieving of their mother's death. They will let me know when the time is right and then we'll make that decision."

The dish of stew, a salad and bread were set upon the table. Franklin blessed the food and their time together.

Gladys brought the conversation back to Martin. "Tell us, Martin, what has been happening in your life?"

"Following Jack's death and my not getting the presidency of Supreme Foods, I was so depressed that I wanted out of our marriage. I wanted to hide, to escape life. This I did, but without the desired effect. I took a dismal room in the heart of Bloomfield to escape. The one-room apartment was so terrible I had to escape it. I'd go across the street to a park where I thought I could be alone. I found out we cannot hide from life," he continued. "I still live there, but that is another story.

"Also coming to the park was a wheelchair-bound psychologist with offices in the church on the other side of the park. It was a desperate time for me. She tried to invite me out of myself. I refused. Then one day, when the clouds were heavy and threatening, we were the only two people in the park. It began to rain. She started to wheel herself back to the church. When she came to where I was sitting she said, 'Sir, would you help me back to my office?' It was my first invitation to life. Like two young kids laughing and playing, we raced as fast as I could push her. We had just gotten inside the church when the rain came down in torrents. I was imprisoned. That was the beginning of a relationship that has grown and opened me to life. I had resigned from Supreme Foods, but they invited me back. Things began opening up for me. I felt good for what I was doing to help others. A couple of days ago I took Dr. Beatrice Bonner to see the colors of autumn. We ended up at our farm. It was then I saw the basketball backboard and hoop. What resulted was I was stopped from what I wanted to do. Beatrice asked me if I had some unfinished business that I needed to attend to. I told her about Jack, my missing seeing him off to service because I was drunk and that, in my grieving, I asked for a divorce. I realized that I needed to be forgiven for my absence from you in your time of grieving. I'm here to ask for your forgiveness."

Gladys got up from her chair and came to Martin. He stood up and they embraced, being dissolved in tears. Martin reached in his hip pocket, removing a clean handkerchief and handing it to Gladys, who dried her eyes. She gave the handkerchief back to Martin. He dried his tears.

Gladys spoke, "Thank you, Martin. That's a gift I shall value my whole life. We cannot bring Jack back, but we can honor his memory in the fullness of each of our lives. A burden has been washed away. Thank you." She reached up and planted a kiss on his cheek.

Martin could not believe the rush of positive feeling he experienced from the embrace and the forgiveness from Gladys. "If we could have had such a relationship when we were married," he thought. "Why did I think having so much centered around myself mattered? So much of what I thought I needed was of little value. I'm amazed at my feeling for Gladys just now. I care about her as I might care for a sister if I ever had one." He turned to talk to both Gladys and Franklin. "May I bless the two of you? Franklin, you'll be blessed with this woman. I regret that I never fully understood what I had. But what I've just now discovered is that even I have been blessed with her love. I do want to have my new friend know the two of you." He paused. "Now, didn't we say something about stew?"

Franklin passed the dish laden with Gladys' special stew to

Martin. Martin held the dish before his face to relish the aroma. "Oh, do I remember this stew? How did the forces of nature know that we'd be together at this moment and that I would be served one of my favorite dishes?"

At last Franklin had a chance to speak. "Thank you, Martin. You've given us a wonderful gift. I do care very much for Gladys. In time we will become a family more fully. For now we'll find ways to grow in our love. Now, Martin, don't hold that stew forever. I, for one, enjoy her stew, too"

Martin spooned some of the stew on his plate before passing it to Gladys. The meal began in earnest. Martin held a bite in his mouth to fully savor the taste then added, "Just as I remembered it. Next time I'll let you know when I'm coming so you'll be sure to have this again. Isn't it interesting how such a little thing as stew can suddenly mean so much? I'm finding that it's the little things that give such value to my life. I must enjoy each experience and find the joy within it. You both have given me great joy this day. I came anxious for what I needed to do for me. I was afraid I would be rejected. When I found Gladys reading and inviting children to be the characters in 'Charlotte's Web', I thought things might be safe. When she saw me and smiled I felt a warmth. Then inviting me to share a dinner with the two of you was the whipping cream on a piece of pie!"

Gladys suddenly exclaimed, "Pie! Whipped cream? Didn't you smell the peach pie cooking in the oven? Thank you, Martin, for reminding me I'm baking a pie for dessert!" She quickly moved to the oven, removing the golden crusted pie. "Whipped cream or ice cream?" she asked.

"Neither for me, love. I want to just enjoy the taste of the pie." Franklin volunteered.

"Same for me, unless you have whipped cream going to waste, and I'd probably spell waste 'w-a-i-s-t'." Martin added, bringing a smile to everyone's face. Gladys cut generous pieces, adding a bit of whipped cream to Martin's piece. In no time the meal was done, not a crumb was left on the table.

"It's a long drive back to Bloomfield, so I must get started on my way. Being with the two of you has been a blessing. Thank you, Gladys, for the forgiveness. This day will remain a most important day in my life."

The three of them stood up and engaged in a group embrace. Martin bid his good-byes and began his trip home. Several times on the trip back to Bloomfield he felt the power of love, love as the initiator of acceptance. He couldn't get back soon enough to share with Beatrice how once more her wisdom had helped him to open to life. And even without a cloudburst! But here was the element of moisture in their tears brought together in a handkerchief. Strange how even love transcends tears!

Chapter 19

Return to Bloomfield

The return to Bloomfield was an interesting dichotomy of his thoughts. A part of the trip seemed to go very fast because he felt so good about the experience with Gladys and Franklin. On the other hand if seemed to take too long because he couldn't wait to share the experience with Beatrice.

It was already late when he parked his car in the apartment garage. He struggled with the question of whether he should call Beatrice or not because of the hour. He rushed to his room to find Ray asleep. Even though he was being very quiet, Martin's exuberance broke the stillness of the night.

Ray stirred. "Do you have to make your excitement so loud? It's obvious, even though you're trying to be quiet. Everything went well? Okay, let's hear it."

"I'm trying to decide if I should call Beatrice or wait until tomorrow morning," Martin questioned.

"It will still be good news in the morning, won't it? I think she'll like to hear good news tomorrow as well but shared when you're together," Ray countered. "You may tell me. Let it out or you'll burst!"

"I went to Pierce anxious about what I had to do. Several times I stopped along the way trying to decide if I were up to the task. I knew I had to go on. When I got to Pierce, I found Gladys working with children in the library. Her sensitivity in her work with the children was wonderful. I watched her in her work. When she had finished work with the students, she approached me with a handshake and a warm greeting. I wanted to take her out to dinner. Instead she invited me to her house for a stew dinner with her new friend, Franklin Pierce, a descendant for which the town was named. Her stew is a marvel to taste. In the discussion that followed, I confessed that I had not been present to her in her time of grieving the death of our son Jack. She got up from her chair and came to me. We embraced, tears running down our cheeks. I handed her my handkerchief. She tried her eyes, returning the handkerchief to me. I dried my tears. She forgave me. Later I thought that even in our tears, when combined in love, brings healing. This day that began in anxiety ended in a most gracious experience. I found the power of love in creating wholeness.

"I will wait until morning when I can be with Beatrice to share the events of this day. Being present with her is much stronger than sharing it over a telephone. Thanks, Ray, for helping me keep a perspective."

Martin removed his clothes down to his boxers, crawled into bed and was soon dreaming of his session with Beatrice. Martin slept soundly. No more anxiety to disturb his rest.

Chapter 20

The Revelation

When Martin awakened, Ray had already finished his morning rituals of showering and shaving and had the box of cornflakes and the milk on the table. "He'll be surprised at the choices he has," Ray thought. "Should I wake him or let him dream away? I think I'll let him dream!"

Ray quietly poured his bowl of corn flakes. The soft sound of flakes being poured was enough to stir Martin. With a husky voice he spoke, "Let me guess the gourmet offering for this day. Oh, yes, I remember, you imported the prize corn from Iowa, had it shipped to Michigan to be made into that wonderful breakfast treat. And the cows? Let's see, cows milked by hand with the richest quality needed for this sumptuous meal?"

Martin threw back the covers, pulled himself out of bed. The sound of the shower caused Ray to sing loudly "Eency, weency spider when up the water spout." The shower suddenly stopped with Martin poking his head out the door, "You know how to cut a man's shower short. I must find someone who can teach you a new song, something to save humanity!"

Martin dressed himself in his finest casual clothes and rushed to the table. "I can hardly wait to share with Beatrice my experience of yesterday. Are you going to be at the restaurant today doing your thing? I was thinking taking Beatrice there might be the right place to share with her my good news. Perhaps a late breakfast or brunch would be good. I can see us now in one of those secluded booths having this intimate conversation."

Ray interrupted, "So it's the intimate you're thinking about? There's life in the old geezer yet! I can't think of a better place for finding life!"

They finished their corn flakes and milk. Martin picked up the phone and called Beatrice. A cheery hello followed. "Oh it's you, Martin. I thought about you all day yesterday and wondered how it all went for you. I trust it was a good day?"

"I can't wait to tell you. My bowl of corn flakes just doesn't cut it this morning. How about meeting me for a late breakfast? It was such a powerful day. How about our having an early brunch, say about 8:30? I'll come by the church and we'll go to the restaurant from there." The plan was settled. Martin, in his excitement, poured another bowl of cornflakes. "Now why did I do that?" he thought. "Do you know what you're doing, Roberts? Get a hold of yourself. You can't blow this one!"

It seemed the clock could not turn fast enough. He paced the floor and finally put on a light jacket and returned to the park. This time he was aware of the newly watered grass and plants, the birds singing their morning songs, and the entrance of a few children with their mothers coming to exercise on the play equipment. Life was rich and beautiful. He kept looking at his watch to be sure to be at the church at 8:30 or perhaps a few minutes earlier. "Will she know what is going through my thick head?" he wondered.

At exactly 8:20 he left his seat in the park and wanted to skip to the church, but a grown man skipping? At least his heart could be skipping. He looked at his watch. Eight twenty eight. He had barely gotten to the church when Beatrice came wheeling out the door. She was obviously excited to see him. Martin bent down and hugged and kissed her.

"Wow!" she said. "You look like you might pop!"

Martin's smile covered his whole face. "Later! But you better be ready!" With that he got behind her and began pushing her to his favorite restaurant. When they arrived, the manager greeted them, looked at their expressions and added, "I would guess that a secluded booth would be required this morning?"

"Right on, man!" Martin added. They were seated in a quiet booth. Ray had already arrived at his post in the window where his easel and art supplies rested. He had clear view of Martin and Beatrice. He closely observed their booth and the couple. He turned his easel so he could face them without their being aware of what he was doing. "Anyway," he thought, "they're so much into each other they'll never be aware of me and what I'll be doing. He began sketching.

Dotty approached the booth asking, "And what may I serve the two of you? How about some orange juice? We also have grapefruits, tomato, and apple juice. Our special this morning is blueberry pancakes. That with a couple of strips of bacon would fill your needs. Or perhaps none of those things would be important," she said as she watched the expressions on their faces.

Beatrice began, "I'd just like an English muffin and a cup of decaf coffee. This is our second breakfast, I imagine."

"I'll make it simple. Same for me," Martin said, eager to get on with his story. The waitress left aware she had intruded on a special time. She quietly served the coffee, muffins and vanished.

Martin reached across the table taking Beatrice's hand in his. "It turned out to be a most marvelous day. I started out fearful of what might happen. I think I was afraid that Gladys would reject me and I might not experience forgiveness. I stopped several times on the trip to Pierce with the excuse of needing a cup of coffee, but in reality I was stalling, not wanting to do what I knew I had to do."

Beatrice listened, her eyes a combination of compassion and anxiety.

"I finally found her at the public library working with young children. She was reading E. B. White's *Charlotte's Web* and then having the students dramatize the event she had just read. It was a most caring experience. I was becoming aware of the Gladys I never knew, although I knew of her love of books." He sipped at his coffee as if to remember details.

"And then?" Beatrice squeezed his hand gently.

Martin continued, "Once she glanced up at me and smiled. When she finished and the children left, she put her things away and then came to me with a warm handshake and greeting. She asked why I had returned to Pierce. I told her I had unfinished business that I had to attend to and that I wanted to take her out to dinner so we could talk. She told me her friend Franklin Pierce was coming over for dinner and that she had made a stew. I do remember the taste of her stew."

"And?"

"We talked a lot about their lives, their coming together as she was helping Franklin be a single parent following his wife's death. She added that Franklin had asked her to move in and live with him, which she said was not yet the right time, until his children had fully grieved their mother's death. And then she confronted me with what had happened in my life."

"Go on. I'm listening," Beatrice smiled, looking at Martin with caring.

"I told her of my deep depression following my not becoming president of Supreme Foods and Jack's death and, that in my depression, I had asked for a divorce. I shared with her how you had invited me to life, and that when we had been together, I saw the basketball backboard and hoop which stopped what I wanted. I didn't tell her that you said when the kiss was interrupted 'Is that all there is?' but that I found I needed to come to her to tell how ashamed I was that I had not been with her in her time of grieving with Jack's death. I asked for her forgiveness. She simply rose from her chair and came to me. We embrace with both of us crying."

"Yes, yes, go on," Beatrice smiled at him. "Yes, yes, go on."

"I handed her my clean handkerchief to dry her tears. She handed it back to me and I dried my eyes. Later I thought of those combined tears and how in the midst of tears in a handkerchief, healing can take place when given in love. I thought of Gladys not so much as my former wife but how I might feel if she were a sister I never had. In the experience of deep anxiety, when love is present, healing and wholeness can result." Martin left his side of the table and joined Beatrice at her side.

"Thank you, love, for loving me back to life," and with that he put his arms around her and kissed her fully.

"Now that's more life it," she said with a blush. "I'm so pleased with the risks you have taken and the ways you have given yourself and continue to give yourself to others."

Martin sat deep in thought. It was as though energy flowed from each hand, one to the other. After a time, Beatrice asked, "A penny for your thoughts!'

Martin remained silent for a moment longer as if he were shaping a question to ask or some statement to share with Beatrice. Then he turned and looked directly to her. "I can't seem to fully understand what is happening in my life. Why am I feeling so 'with it'? I've seldom felt so satisfied with my life. What do you observe is happening to me?"

Beatrice paused, "I hate to break the mood I'm feeling, but since you asked, I'll try to explain what I think has happened."

She reflected intently before answering. "If you're asking the psychologist, dear, I think it's best described as 'Pathways to Wholeness,' a model for growth described in psychological and theological terms. You have been changing every moment since the cloudburst and we raced to the church to avoid being drenched. You began working through old, useless memories and adopting more productive ways of relating to people and the world about you."

Martin's feelings for this woman were overwhelming him. She reflected on his attempt to kiss her but which was interrupted when he saw the basketball court his wife Gladys had installed for their son, Jack, and his practice. Beatrice was disappointed by the interruption. She was aware of his need to have closure with his former wife, Gladys.

Dotty came carrying the blueberry pancakes, strips of bacon and decaf coffee. "I thought a bit of fresh fruit would top it off" she said. "Enjoy your brunch." She left smiling as she looked at the drawing taking shape at Ray's easel. "That man of mine is something special. That couple will be pleased. He's captured the inner joy they are experiencing. Dear me, I forgot they only wanted a muffin and decaf coffee! See what even seeing special love can do to one's memory?" she said to herself.

Beatrice began sharing her thought while sipping a bit of coffee or munching a strip of bacon. "When you saw Gladys working with the children and you observed the loving way she related to them, you saw something that you had not seen before. When she invited you to her home for dinner and you saw the special relationship she had established with her friend, you probably reflected on the openness you were finding in other relationships. That only pressed you on to your need to move forward in your life. All of that was evidence of unconditional acceptance or grace." She paused to think through what he had shared. She held his hand more firmly.

"When you risked sharing with her your feelings of not being present to her in her grief at your son's death, she was moved by a part of you she had not known before. She was probably aware of the struggle you must have had and was moved to express her caring for you. When you embraced and tears flowed, there was a new kind of love for each of you."

She looked at Martin. "I was moved by your expression of finding love expressed in a handkerchief and the mingling of tears. Martin, that is a beautiful story. Would that all relationships, if they must come to an end, have such a touching expression." She put down her napkin and silverware and leaning toward him said, "It's now my turn." She put her arms about his neck and drew him to her. "And I don't want to hear, 'Is that all there is?'" With that she planted a passionate kiss on his lips.

"Oh, darn," Ray shouted in a loud whisper, as he came to their table with his drawing of them. "If you'd had just started with that I could have made the picture even more passionate!" He laid his art on the table before them. His girlfriend raced back to the booth with a fresh pot of decaf.

Beatrice and Martin laid the sketch across the table marveling at the depth of expression Ray had caught.

"I thought you might need something to help you remember this day. I hope you recognize the two lovers in this picture," he said with joy erupting. "I'm sorry to eavesdrop in on your conversation. Although I couldn't hear a word that was said, the artist in me felt more than could be said in words. You are both a blessing to me in my life."

Beatrice asked, "I wonder if we could get fresh cups of coffee and another blueberry pancake?"

Remembering a telephone call she added, "Oh, by the way, Martin, you had a call from Mr. James. He has some good news for you, something about a cafe at their plant. He wants you to come by today. Sorry to interrupt."

New cups of coffee were poured. More pancakes arrived. Dotty replied, "I guess no additional stimulus is needed," she said with a knowing smile.

Ray brought the wheelchair to the table. Martin helped Beatrice to the chair. They put their arms about the two admirers, thanking them for what they had given them.

Martin asked, "Ray, could your bring the sketch home with you? I'm taking Beatrice back to her office and I don't want anything to happen to your work, although I would doubt that I need anything else to remind me of this moment except a frame."

Martin began pushing Beatrice on her way back to her office at the church. Their walk back to her office was light and joyous. Martin was beginning, for the first time in his life, to know the many kinds of love. As he pushed he thought, "Why must I take so long to discover love? Is this a part of each of our lives? Must we know the depth of sorrow and loss to find the height of joy?"

A new dimension in his life was taking shape... aspects of being he had not known. As he looked down at her soft blond hair he wondered about the depth of her awareness and just how she acquired it. It was something greater than words inscribed in a textbook. "Am I learning something about love I had never experienced before?"

His inner thoughts continued. "How could she know almost my every thought? Why was she able to risk actions when I was aware of my fear of being vulnerable? Was the passionate kiss at the restaurant a new dimension in our lives? Where will all these new discoveries take us?"

The questions raced on in his mind. "Will she be a part of my life beyond her being a psychologist? A worker in the church? How and when will I find the awareness?"

He felt the growing relationship with Beatrice. "This I'm discovering. All things ripen in their own time."

Martin pushed her to the church and to her office. He leaned down to embrace her and kiss her warmly. He thought, "And there wasn't even a cloudburst!"

Chapter 21

Back at the Office

In a short time they were back at her office. Neither of them wanted this time together to end, although they were unsure of just how to express that feeling.

As he made his way out of the church, the secretary called to him, "Mr. Roberts, a Mr. James called to ask you to come to his office. Oh, yes, and he asked that you bring Mr. Wynn with you."

Martin rushed back to the restaurant and invited Ray to join him. "Mr. James wants to see you, too."

"What more can happen to make this day such a joy?" he thought. He could hardly contain himself, so excited was he to have had such positive experience yesterday and the beginning of this day. Hopefully his good luck would continue. What he had yet to totally comprehend is that people set themselves up often for their good fortune. He had already learned that the opposite or the distressing "luck" is often of one's own doing. Would his suggestion of the Cafe On Line and his desire to have all employees have a stake in the work of the company be accepted? And what were some of the first issues to be considered? Would they have additional pictures of grandmother James collected and could those be shared with Ray for some marketing tasks? So many details to be thought about.

When he arrived at Supreme Foods with Ray, he quickly parked his car and rushed to the administrative offices.

Entering the office, he greeted the secretary. "Good morning, Miss Franks. How's your day going? No Mr. Garrett and my dumb entrance to embarrass myself ? You were wonderful on Thursday. Mr. Garrett really enjoyed the exchange you and I had while in his presence. Does making myself such a goof ball make me seem human?"

"The two Mr. James have been talking about your ideas and seem excited about them. I think they'd like you to just go on in. By the way you had a call from someone from the Kroger Company.

They asked if you knew a Mr. Randall Garrett? They said they'd call back when you were here."

"Thank you, Miss Franks," Martin replied.. "Hmmm. I wonder what that might be about."

Martin loosened the tie about his neck, caught a deep breath and knocked at Mr. James' office door. "Come in, Martin. Would you like something to drink? Leland and I have been talking about your proposal of the First Line Cafe or whatever we'll call it. We've also talked with the chairs of each of the departments. Everyone seemed very interested in the idea, especially how the employees in the various departments can become involved and have a sense of investment in the company. I'm sorry, Mr. Wynn, welcome to Supreme Foods. I get so centered on a project that I often forget my manners. Grandmother James would frown on such a behavior. I'm not sure what my father would have done! I'm looking forward to your helping us make this a most inviting space. By the way, you'll need to go check in at the Human Services Department and get started on the payroll."

Ray could hardly contain his excitement. It was all he could do to stand still, with a smile so great he feared he would explode. It took over his whole face. He couldn't wait to be excused to do the paperwork and become a part of the company.

Jimmy's son Leland followed, "I'm particularly interested in the creative aspect of the plan, and how we can get employees interested in developing new products and ways of using our products in new, imaginative ways. As a matter of fact, that is where my interests lie. I think it was something that I acquired when I was working with the students at Lily Wong's Cooking School. It will be interesting to see how the employees take hold and become more involved with creating products for sale. Your suggestion of awarding shares caught their ears. That's brilliant, Martin."

His father quickly added, "They were suggesting that a dining space be on the street side where the general public can visit and partake in the product approval process. We'll need to construct or remodel space.

"There will need to be permits arranged with the city, and we'll have to apply for a license to conduct a dining facility. Your ideas are great. Thank you, Martin. All this puts marketing on a new plane! Let's get started! Martin, I'd like you to work with Ray Wynn and draw up some plans for the space. The two of you are to begin the study of possible spaces. Leland, would you oversee the permits needed? Since we're not into such activities regularly, we will need an architect to create the final plans. I'd like this all to be completed in time for an opening before Thanksgiving."

"Amazing! And this is October already? No grass will grow under our feet!" Martin replied. "We're ready!"

Ray followed, "We can do it, Mr. James. And thank you for your trust in me. I will give it everything I can. Martin, I'm ready. Let's go!"

As they walked out the administration offices, Martin suggested they ask Paul Wright to join them.

"Come on, Martin, we have a job to do."

They went to the Shipping Department and invited Paul to join them. They went to the front of the building and suggested that the First Line Cafe be close to the central Administrative offices. They wanted to make sure that the general public knew of the relationship and purpose of the Cafe was related to the mission of Supreme Food Products, Inc. Paul suggested that the current file room for the administration be moved further back in the building but close enough to the administration and that space could be developed into a kitchen and a center for creating new food products and meals for employees and the public.

Paul added, "The parking along the front of the building would accommodate customers coming to the Cafe. Employees of Supreme Foods could find parking in an area closer to their area of work but away from the Cafe. Internal hallways within the company would all lead to the Cafe."

Martin said, "Very good thinking, Paul. We'll report this to Leland, who can hire those who would draw up the plans and secure the permits from the city. I'm sure Mr. James would like this done before Thanksgiving, but that may not happen knowing how city offices work and the complexity of the work to be done."

Ray continued the conversation. "I'd like to travel to the farms where Grandmother James began the work that developed into Supreme Foods. I hear that the 640 acres have remained pretty much as they were when she was initiating her work. I know it's probably too late to go there today, but perhaps we could go visit the farms tomorrow? Anyway, I have a painting session with Dotty tonight."

"That would fit right in to where I want to take our plans. Let's do it. We can get up early tomorrow morning and be there to see the farm in action. Great idea, Ray," Martin responded.

Martin and Ray each went their own way, Martin to the church with hope of seeing Beatrice, and Ray to follow his passion for painting. He had begun a painting of Dotty in the nude. Each felt good about how their lives were opening up with the new relationships. They felt so good about the present, they trusted themselves to their futures.

Chapter 22

A Painting session

Ray left Supreme Foods for Dotty's apartment…and the painting session. Many times, while in college, he had painted nudes, models hired to pose for the students. In his wildest dreams he was not prepared for what was to happen at this session.

Dotty disrobed as Ray was putting paint on his palette, setting up his easel, and putting his painter smock on. Turpentine and the smell of oil and paint excited him.

Dotty had brushed her hair to fall in the same places she remembered it being in the previous session. Ray did go to her and adjust it slightly as she prepared to find her place on the padded table space, her back to Ray and her upper body turned upward to reveal her youthful breasts.

Ray studied her body and was satisfied that it was much like the previous sessions. He began painting. As he painted, he became aware of this session having emotions he had not fully known previously. He felt his own body responding to his feeling. He tried to suppress the feeling but it would not work. "I'm sorry, Dotty, I simply cannot continue. Let's take a break."

Dotty turned her whole body that she could see Ray. She was fully aware of the distension in his trousers. Getting up from her place she came to Ray in all her nudity. She took the palette and the brushes from his hands and placed them on the table where his other art supplies were. Then she reached up and removed his painter's smock from his body. That followed with her unbuttoning the sleeves of his shirt and the button on the front of his shirt. She pulled the shirt tails from his pants, taking the shirt from him and laying it on the place where she had lain. She backed away admiring his chest and upper body. Then she reached down and unbuckled his belt and zipped down the fly on his pants. Ray removed his shoes and socks. When they were fully free she pushed his pants to the floor. Ray obliged by stepping out of his pants. She took his undershirt and rubbed his chest before pushing his shorts down around his feet. Not a word was said. Silence was profound. Ray had never experienced anything as powerful as her disrobing him.

Taking his hand in hers she led him to her bedroom where they made love as only lovers can. Afterwards, came the most wonderful sleep he could ever remember.

Sunrise came too early. It was almost seven o'clock when they awakened.

"Heaven help us. I'm supposed to be meeting with Martin to go with him to the James farms.

It's almost the time that I should be there. Can you drive me to Supreme Foods, love?"

They jumped into their clothes and hurried to Dotty's car and off to Supreme Foods. Martin was standing by his car waiting for Ray. As Ray got out of the car and headed toward Martin's car, Martin said, "Now I know why you didn't sleep in your own bed last night. I thought you were having a painting session last evening?"Martin said as Ray approached the car. "What was the subject being painted? Were you into a nude subject?"

"It seems you're getting a little personal. Yes, I was working on the nude painting of Dorothy."

"Oh, so it's Dorothy now? When did the "Dotty" name get dropped.? And how did the painting go?"

"I have painted many nudes before. They were all hired models posing for us. I felt no attachment with any of them. They were all just bodies with light and shadows, shapes and colors. Last night started that way but then something began happening to me. I don't have to tell another man what that was all about. Not since I was in my late teens and early twenties have I been caught up with such passion. I don't have to tell you the rest of the story, unless you're partially dead." Ray stopped that conversation and got into Martin's car. "Let's get going. My story is over. Anyway, I need to see where Grandmother James began what became Supreme Foods."

They arrived at the farms just as they had completed milking the cows, and the milk was being processed to become rounds of cheese at the cheese barn. They borrowed an all terrain vehicle and toured each of the 160 acre farms. At last they returned to the main building where Grandmother James lived. The building was rather large to accommodate her large family. Many of the antique pieces she used in her kitchen were still hanging there. While some things were modified to accommodate the needs of the present call for supplies, much was kept in its original places. All this made a deep impression on Martin. He thought of what he would propose to Mr. James for future use of the farms.

Ray made careful notes of the use of utensils and how they had been displayed. There was no question but that they were housed to accommodate the elderly lady with a lot of work to be done. If they were still being used, how they were being used was still efficient, and so remained where they had been arranged earlier.

Notes having been taken and memories fresh in mind, the two men headed back to the administration offices of Supreme Foods.

As they were ushered into Mr. James' office, Ray enthusiastically volunteered, "That was a most wonderful day. There was little we missed. I can well imagine that the First Line Cafe might be decorated in a manner like that of Grandmother James' home. Obviously she was a most efficient woman. Otherwise, how could she have fed and cared for her large family and have had time to serve customers. I saw many patterns that I hope will become a part of our future cafe."

It was Martin who excitedly followed Ray. "Seeing the farm

and how so much of it has been preserved in Grandmother James period, we may build on it. I kept thinking of those farms as a working museum. With all the bedroom communities being built and so many things being created with contemporary motives, there may come a time when youth will need to visit such a place to discover what went on before the things they have and do today."

Mr. James brightened at Martin's suggestion. "That's a wonderful idea, Martin. I will talk this over with the rest of the family. For example, I like the idea that students could come and see cheese being made. We might even have some of the cows being milked by hand and some being milked by mechanical means. Students might even try their hand at milking. All the things that became a part of the early days of the company could be viewed and experienced. Students could experience in a 'hands on' way what life was like at an earlier period in this community. Can't you just imagine girls using some of Grandmother James' recipes, doing their own cooking and marketing what they had made? Martin, you're a wonder. I'm so grateful you're a part of the Supreme Foods team. Grandmother James would be smiling from ear to ear!"

"Once the First Line Cafe is completed, you'll see Grandmother James smile," Martin added. "I doubt that we'll make the Cafe by Thanksgiving but we'll give it our best." With Mr. James being pleased, Martin and Ray excused themselves to begin the refining of plans for the in-house restaurant.

As the day wore on and it became time to stop working, Ray had trouble staying focused on his work at the company. He thought, "What will today bring? Do I go back with Dorothy to continue the painting session? Will I be expecting a repeat of last evening? What is it that drives the actions of Dotty? Of my actions? What is the full meaning of last evening? Where is it taking us? What if she gets pregnant?" Ray was bedeviled by the questions filling his mind.

It was all a worthless questioning. As they left the building, there in her car sat Dorothy smiling a warm greeting. "Hello, Martin. How did your day go? My work at the restaurant was most fun. I can't remember a day when I felt so good in working with customers! The whole day was so relaxing."

Martin could not understand the purpose of the questions in his mind. "Do we need to explain the 'why' of all of that?" A part of Martin wanted to be sure that what Ray was experiencing was in his best interest. There was also a part of him that wanted to be sure that Ray would be present for his purpose of building Supreme Foods. That was that old part of Martin centered on his own advancement. Old patterns of behaviors do not die easily. He watched Ray slide into the passenger seat of Dotty's car, watched them exchange kisses and go dashing off for their painting session. Or was it to be more than a time for painting?

When Ray and Dotty arrived at her apartment, she quickly undressed for her posing. A suggestive look at Ray went unnoticed as he donned his painter's smock and prepared his brushes and palette for their session. Dorothy assumed her most suggestive position, trying to excite Ray for what she anticipated would be repeated this evening.

Ray saw the full message. He chose to ignore the invitation. "Not tonight, dear. Last night was special and I found it to be a wonderful experience. I am an artist and I must hold to my purpose of painting. If I succumb to those physical pleasures before I complete my work, I may defeat all that I am capable of being. Thank you, Dorothy, for your gifts to me," and picking up a brush and his palette he tried to resume his painting.

"It's no use, love. I can't get into my painting. Would you get dressed, please? We need to talk," Ray said with hesitation.

Dotty dressed slowly, with a sense of disappointment. Ray sat himself on a sofa and awaited Dotty coming to his side. When at last she arrived he took her hand in his and looking deeply into her eyes began, "The day we met at the restaurant and you saw my sketch of Martin, was a most wonderful moment. I felt you were in tune with what I was about. And when you invited others to see my work, it was even more special. You invited me to do a drawing of you, and you said you would pay me for it. As a homeless person previous to meeting Martin, the thought of a little money was a wonderful gift."

Dorothy squeezed his hand to acknowledge her memory of the story he was telling.

Ray continued. "As I began a larger portrait and I studied you more deeply, I began to see qualities that are almost impossible for me to put into words but that I could express them on a canvas with paint. Martin, seeing the picture, asked who it was. He could not see what I had seen and I said, 'But you are not an artist'."

She reached over and kissed him on his cheek. "Go on, Ray. Is there more?"

"Oh yes. I do not know why, but I did invite you to model for me in the nude. Always before, while in college, we painted nudes hired to pose for us. I am aware I was seeing light and shadows, colors and curves. I'm not sure why I wanted to paint you in the nude. Probably what we experienced last evening was a part of that, although at the time I was not aware of such thoughts.

"When I interrupted the painting and suggested we take a break you came to me with the most amazing invitation I ever received. That whole experience was unbelievable. It was marvelous for me, for I found the giving of myself to you so completely was something I had never experienced before. There was a part of you I began to know which was in the original portrait I did of you. A part of me wants to get to know you more fully, to find those truths of you hidden within my painting that I find impossible to put into words."

Ray paused as if to find the words to express his inner most feelings. At last he began again, "I do know there is so much of you I need to know. There is much more than what we gave to each other last evening. It is all to be found in the many ways we give ourselves to each other. When I paint in your nude presence, the physical parts intrude upon me. I think I will have to take the painting back to Martin's apartment and continue to work on it there. Perhaps as I surrender my thinking into the Dorothy I know at this time and search for the deeper meaning, I will find what it is that I search for in the depth of our commitment to each other. It is that intimacy that I must find. I'm sure that neither one of us know ourselves fully. Perhaps with each time together, we awaken within each other more of that soul that lies there waiting to be discovered. It is that depth that brings us fullness in life. It does not lie close to the surface of life, but in our commitment to the wholeness of life." Ray turned his whole body to Dorothy and they embraced in a kiss that opened the door to deeper awareness.

Dorothy, looking deeply into Ray's eyes, said. "I understand, at least in part, what you are saying. Can anyone fully understand the ideas and those deeper feeling of another? I, too, want those qualities you describe. Sometimes my urgency for a relationship causes me to shortchange what I truly want. In time, I'm sure we'll find what we search for."

With that Dorothy got up from her place on the sofa and began to reassemble Ray's paints and art supplies. Ray stood up and she took his painter's smock and folded it. In no time all his supplies and the canvas was assembled and prepared to take back to Martin's apartment.

"We'll have to be careful with the painting. The paint has not yet hardened and can easily smear," Ray added. "Dotty, the more I know you the deeper my love for you seems to be growing. You give me full permission to be who I may become to be. That's a very special gift to another person. It invites me to continue to give myself to you."

As they prepared to return to Martin's apartment, they held each other in a most loving and given embrace. The accompanying kiss seemed to awaken their souls.

Ray carefully carried the canvas to the car as Dotty carried the painting supplies. With all the materials securely housed, they got in the car and drove to Martin's apartment.

As they stopped at the entrance to the apartment building, Dotty turned off the motor and, facing Ray, said, "There's a part of me that's jealous that others may see a part of me in your painting even before I can begin to know more of myself. There's a bit of jealousy that others are sharing in your own discoveries of yourself. I do remember reading once that jealousy is only caring that is out of perspective. I do want our caring and love to be open and full of truth. Now let me help you up to the apartment."

With that they got out of the car and began to hike up the stair to Martin's second floor one room apartment. Some of Ray's art work was finding its place on the walls, softening the space. When the materials were in their place, the two lovers once more held each other and then without a word, descended the stairs to her car. Ray opened the door for Dotty to take her place in the driver's seat. "Drive carefully, love." With that she was off to her own apartment.

Chapter 23

Meeting in the Park

Ray awakened early with thoughts of his conversations with his emerging lover. He quietly dressed for his day at Supreme Foods, donned a jacket to ward off the late October frost and crossed the street to the park. He needed time to think through what had taken place last evening. Conflicts in his thinking left him with an internal struggle. There was a strong part of him that wanted the relationship he had with Dotty on that one great evening. There was also the pull for his realizing the purpose of his gift in painting. Previously, when working as an illustrator for a company, he managed art to express an idea laid out before him. When he began painting Dotty there was an added dimension to his painting. He was seeing something that spoke to him more deeply. He could not find the words to express what was, but it was easy to express it in his art. "Is this true with all artists?" he asked himself as he sat there in the morning chill. What was that unknown truth about Dorothy he wanted to discover and put into words? Perhaps that might never happen. None of what was happening could have been planned before it occurred. What forces provided those awakenings?

Ray closed his eyes with the hope that his mind's eye would begin to reveal answers to his questions. All he could see was Dotty seductively lying in her modeling position. He relived the passions he experienced in their togetherness. She was awakening something deep within him. He was so deeply involved in his memory of her, he was not aware Martin had joined him on the bench in the park. What was it that brought these two men together? Was it their awareness that love is the force that was giving them a fuller life?

Martin began the conversation. "I did take a peek at your new painting. Now that spoke to me. Guess I'm not dead yet!"

Ray thought for a moment and then answered, "I'm very confused. I'm sure you know what happened a few evenings ago when I didn't come home. The total surrender of myself to Dotty was a powerful experience. A part of me wants to have an experience like that again. There is another part of me that somehow knows that I'm discovering something of Dotty that I cannot put into words but for me is easily expressed in my painting. I want to know more of her. I somehow fear that just living in the physical part may deny my knowing her at a more significant level. Those two parts of me struggle for my being."

"Boy, do I know that struggle. I am just beginning to learn that struggle." Martin shared after thinking it through for a short time. "I met Gladys when we were just out of our teens. The sexual urge was overwhelming. We experienced sex. It was so satisfying we continued until she became pregnant. I never got much beyond that in our relationship. I also became obsessed with my own work and dreamed of becoming president of the company I worked for. Our son, Jack, was the major thing that kept us together. When Jack was killed in an automobile accident and I wasn't present for Gladys in her grieving, she moved out of our bedroom and into Jack's room. I, in my own self, felt alone. I said 'The magic has gone out of the marriage. I want out.' When I visited Gladys and saw the magic of her working with children I discovered a part of her that had been there probably always but I had not taken time to discover. I now wonder if I had taken the time would our marriage still be intact, and would the history of our family have been different?"

Ray picked up the conversation. "I think you're catching a glimpse of the struggle that I'm feeling. With my relationship with

Dotty, only time will reveal what will shape our lives." He paused. "Okay, let's do go for a bite of breakfast. I must face Dotty and the forces that are shaping our lives."

With that, the two men left their places on the park bench and headed off for their favorite breakfast place. As they entered the restaurant, Dotty saw them and came rushing to them, throwing her arms about Ray and planting a kiss on his mouth before returning to the couple she had been serving.

"My, oh my, is this a service afforded all male customers? If so, I feel cheated. I never received such a welcome." said the bald headed man of the elderly couple Dotty was serving.

With that she bent over and planted a ruby-red lipstick kiss on the top of his head. "Don't complain that you're treated unfairly in this restaurant. I'd give you a hug but you're sitting down." With that the gentleman quickly got up from his chair and opened his arms. Dotty playfully responded with a hug.

Ray was watching the entire encounter and thinking, "But that's Dotty, enjoying life to its fullest and inviting others to a more playful, fun time. Is that one of those qualities that I see in her as I continue to create a painting of her? From that first day I met her she sees the joy of living, a positive part of being. It seemingly comes from the depth of her soul."

Ray was hungry and called to Dotty, "Hey, you gorgeous creature, how about serving two very hungry men at the next table? A guy can't live on a kiss alone! But don't let that word get around too far!"

Dotty turned in the order for the elderly couple and then came to Ray and Martin's table. She sat in the chair facing Ray. "Haven't I seen you somewhere before? You do look familiar. I haven't seen you for a couple of days." Then she thought to herself, "If he'd take off his clothes I think I'd remember him more fully!"

Dotty continued, "And what do two hungry men think will satisfy their greatest needs? Food? That we serve here in an open fashion? Today's special is two hotcakes, two eggs (any style) and two strips of bacon. It can be served pronto, since looking at the clock, I suspect you two have to get on the job without delay. Right?"

Martin, who had quietly observed the whole transaction, replied, "Right! Supreme Foods eagerly anticipates our gifts this day!" It was his way of attempting to continue the playfulness.

They chose the special, and Dotty turned the order in. She returned to the table and seriously turned to Ray, "Why have I not seen you to continue the painting sessions? Have I done something to create a problem for us? I'll pick you up following your work day and we'll continue the session." With that, she got up and went to get the food for the tables and to continue her work, in a sense saying that her decision was final. "Oh, but you took the painting back to your apartment," she said with disappointment.

"Ah, another quality is her ability to take charge of issues. That shows up in my painting of her as personal strength." Ray continued his thoughts. "Strange how much of another person is revealed by looking at the way they relate to others and how that is revealed in a way through a painting. Do other artists grow in the purpose of their art as they more fully know their subjects? How much of myself and the values I hold become revealed in what I put on a canvas? How is it that Dotty is bringing to my awareness so much of what life is about? Is that a quality that invites from each other the potential of each that gives strength to a marriage? And why do I raise the question of marriage in my relationship with Dotty? What are the forces that bring two people together? It sometimes feels like Nature is making decisions for us, something that lies beyond our conscious thinking."

Martin and Ray finished their breakfast, greeted the elderly couple at the next table, paid their bill, and left a tip for Dotty. A quick embrace with Dotty and they were on their way.

Dotty reminded them, "Remember, I'm picking you up, Ray, at the end of your day! Will it be a new beginning?"

Chapter 24

Supreme Foods Agenda

As Martin and Ray pulled into the parking lot they were greeted by Leland,who arrived at the same time. They parked their cars and headed for their offices.

"Morning, guys. I just came from meeting with the architect and discussing plans for the "On Line" Cafe. I shared the report you and Paul provided for us. The architect seemed to think it will work without any serious problems. She's planning to come to our offices later this morning. I hope the two of you will join us to share your thinking,"

Martin replied, "You know we'll be there. Much will hopefully come from this new venture. We'll be interested in what he'll have to say."

Leland answered, "It's a 'she'. Bonnie Bright has a great reputation for designing restaurants. I think you'll be amazed with her thinking. I expect her about eleven this morning. We'll meet with her, and then take her out to lunch at a place of her choosing. Her choice of a desirable ambiance will give us clues to her thinking. She may even decide to share with us a restaurant she has designed." With that Leland rapped at his father's door and entered to share the efforts of his morning.

"Good morning, Miss Franks. We didn't mean to ignore you.

The ideas of our On Line Cafe are taking some precedence. Are there any messages for us?" Martin inquired.

"As a matter of fact, one of Mr. James' family brought a number of snapshots of Grandmother James which you requested. They are greatly valued and they wish to have then back," Miss Franks explained as she deposited them in a folder.

Martin replied, "We'll give these to Ray, who will be doing some illustrative work based on Grandmother James' history and pictures." He accepted the folder and handed it on to Ray. They walked on to Martin's office, that they might have a drawing ready when the Cafe is completed.

Ray settled into a comfortable chair and began looking at the pictures of Grandmother James that one of the grandchildren had shared. After quickly scanning each picture, he went to a table and began laying out each picture to determine if there was something that suggested a quality that became pervasive. At last he found several that seemed to suggest a wholesome quality and a determined look about her.

"Martin, come take a look. What do you see when you glance at these photos?" Ray asked.

"Hmmm. My first impression is the friendly quality, and a relaxed family feeling, like she cared about people and things in her life. In her picture with others in her family, there is some kind of almost reverence for her. She seems to be in charge without being 'one-way' about it," Martin replied in studying the group. "I feel drawn to her."

"What do you want done with these pictures?" Ray asked. "Knowing you, I would guess you have something very articulate in mind!"

"I remember with some pain, my rejection when applying for the presidency of Supreme Foods. I thought having capital gains was what was important, that we could downsize and lower quality to increase profit, but I was told that when Grandmother James began what became Supreme Foods, it was the quality that mattered most. When we visited the Shipping Department and Paul gave us a package that was to be shipped, I looked at the printing and imagined a design with Grandmother James' picture and the words 'A Grandmother James' Quality'. Is that something you could create?"

"Does water flow downhill? Is Supreme Foods a quality company? Let me at it! I'll have several options before the restaurant is opened. Knowing you that will be a beginning test for the members of the staff," Ray added. He was beginning to anticipate Martin's ideas.

At about a quarter of eleven Leland called his father, Martin, and Ray to his office. "I want us to be ready for Miss Bright. We need to make full use of her time. This I know, she can be right on time," Leland volunteered.

At exactly eleven, Miss Franks knocked on the door, and Leland opened it and ushered in Miss Bright. All the men caught their breath, for before them stood this most petite and beautiful young woman. Her beautiful auburn hair cascaded down over her shoulders. Her refined features seemed to imply that she was able to qualify for Miss America. One could almost imagine this sweet young voice gently addressing them.

A low, loud voice interrupted the scene. "All right, you guys, let's get down to business. We have much to explore before I'm to take you to a restaurant that I've had my hand in! Tell me again, just what is the intent of the space being considered? "

Leland, introducing Martin said, "This is Martin Roberts, our key staff person in charge of Marketing. With him is his friend Mr. Ray Wynn, the artist. Oh, yes I guess I'd better introduce my father, Jimmy James, otherwise I might be disinherited. Men, this is Miss Bonnie Bright. I've frequented restaurants she has designed. I've been impressed." He stopped as if to change his thinking.

"Martin, you proposed the idea, why don't you share your thinking?"

Martin looked off into space as if collecting his thoughts. "Would you like the short or the long version?"

In her low forceful voice, "The long version but short enough that I can take you all to lunch!" she said in a playful tone.

Martin adjusted himself in his chair, took a long breath and began, "I'm aware that participants in an activity are more fully engaged in the activity if they have ownership in the activity. Production increases. We are talking about how we increase employees' ownership and invite their own creativity to developing new products. The question is how to be creative, field test products and prepare those products for the market? One way is to become involved in decisions regarding what they prepare for the market. Having a kitchen that prepares foods to serve employees, and at the same time asking the employees to approve the products, seems like a meaningful way of developing ownership. Employees would be invited to make suggestions on the preparation of foods and the look of packaging that would invite buyers to try the products. The cafe would also be open to the public with their responding to the quality and appearance of the packaging." Martin stopped to think of what to say next.

"Thinking creatively about foods can be a rich part of using individual items in fresh new ways, a part of marketing. Perhaps an outgrowth might be publications of recipes, magazines and cook books. It is the Betty Crocker system, but now applied to a local plant and a local community."

He thought a moment and then continued. "We must create the image that reflects the very basis on which the company is based. Do people know how the James family has kept alive that which Grandmother James began years ago? We must create a process to further her dedication to quality products, while at the same time empowering all people who relates to Supreme Food Products in some way."

Miss Bright readjusted her position on her chair and then replied, "If you carry this concept further, you may well change production processes. If quality is more important than return on investment, it may well establish a new direction in production and marketing. I like what I am hearing and I may require more hours of thinking through the processes and how that gets translated into bricks and mortar. Let me think about this more. Even an architect needs time for empowerment. When I'm heavy into thinking my stomach begins to growl, or is it that it's lunch time? Follow me. We'll be going to the Marley Hotel main dining room that overlooks the golf course!"

`Martin, thinking to himself, "I've often wondered who designed that restaurant? It really meets its purpose of connecting the hotel to the golf course. Even as one is hungry for dessert, that feeling is easily delayed by the desire to get out on the greens. Even if one is not a golfer, one can enjoy watching others in their engagement and enjoyment of the game."

All four men, without expressing their surprise, were caught up in the directness and the purposefulness of Miss Bright's attention to details of the discussions. Probably each thought without saying it, "No wonder she's so effective in her work. She catches men by surprise by her ability to stay focused and centered on the tasks to be done."

Miss Bright continued. "We'll go in my car. It may be a bit cozy with five aboard but it will afford us time for discussion, to continue our conversations. Sometimes a chance statement triggers significant thoughts and we want all to be present in the genesis of ideas."

Within minutes they all piled into her car and were on their way to the Marley Hotel.

Chapter 25

At the Marley Hotel

Conversations on the way to the Marley were almost nonexistent. It seemed that everyone was deep in thought of what might develop at their meeting in the Marley dining room. Arriving at the parking lot in front of the hotel, all got out, with Ray quickly opening the driver's door and assisting in Miss Bright's emergence. One could readily see, by response, she was independent and able to attend to her own needs.

Slightly embarrassed by their lack of conversation, Leland began with, "Did you design the dining area here at the Marley?" It seemed like a safe way to open the discussion. Everyone seemed deeply in thought concerning how to get answers to the questions not yet clearly formed in relation to their individual responsibilities.

Miss Bright sensed the discomfort. "Let's wait for any questions until we're seated and ordered food. I can think better when I'm less hungry!" Her response seemed to relax the group. They proceeded on to the dining room.

A waiter seeing Martin rushed up to him saying, "Mr. Roberts, are you taking on this whole group on in a game of golf? Congratulations on your game with Mr. Garrett." Suddenly aware that his intrusion was not appropriate, "Excuse me, Mr. Roberts is a familiar face around here. Now may I help you?"

Miss Bright moved forward, taking charge of the lunch arrangements. "We would like a table for the five of us where we can get a good view of the whole dining room and the patterns of movement to and from this space and the ease of service from the kitchen area. Oh, yes, and how the total space addresses the setting of the golf course, which provides a relaxed invitation to other services of the hotel."

"Yes, ma'am. Please follow me." He took them to a table slightly to the left of the center which had a perfect view of the golf course, where they could view customers entering and leaving and a clear view of the passageway to the kitchen at the right of the center.

Ray was thinking to himself, "She's answered many questions already by defining how the various responsibilities of service people function in the space. Some of my questions are already answered."

The waiter presented menus at each setting and then quietly served water glasses. Wine glasses were already in place. He continued, "And what would you like to drink?"

Miss Bright continued, "We have work to accomplish. No alcohol now. That's for after work if it is desired."

Mr. James inserted, "Grandmother James wouldn't approve such drinking on the job!"

Martin thought, "Hmmm, another quality for the image of Grandmother James and what we say about Supreme Foods! I wonder if Ray caught that gentle statement for his artwork?"

"Our specials today are: A prime rib sandwich on our multi-grain bread and a spinach avocado-apple salad with pomegranate dressing. For those wishing a more substantial meal,may I suggest our baked salmon with an orange dressing and a mixed greens salad with a choice of dressings. May I give you a moment to look at the other offerings?"

Miss Bright asserted, "May I have your spinach-avocado-apple salad with the pomegranate dressing, without the sandwich?" Her passion for getting things done seemed to dominate the activities at each step of the session.

"I'd be pleased to serve that. Is anyone else ready?"

Ray replied," I'd like the same salad, but with a slice of your own baked bread."

"Make mine the baked salmon. I'm hungry!" Leland ordered next. "Was the orange dressing one of our Supreme Foods products?"

"I don't know, but I'll ask the chef. Thanks for asking."

In minutes the orders were completed, with Mr. James adding, "I'd like a cup of coffee with my order."

The waiter moved quietly across the dining room to the entrance to the kitchen. Everyone gave their full attention to the movements. Their attention was then directed to a couple entering the dining area and their being greeted and directed to a seating next to the window facing the golf course.

Ray was the first to speak. "Amazing use of space. I admire the efficiency possible by the way the zones are organized. We won't have a golf course to view from our dining area, but we will have purpose for our use of the space. I think, from what everyone is telling me, we have a history and a quality of service to remind us of why we are there."

"Well said, Ray. What you have described is what we must address, the coming and goings of both our employees and the general public. If we are to invite individuals to tell us of ways to increase our service and our products we must accommodate that activity by the way we create displays and means for reporting," Mr. James added.

Miss Bright invited more information for her use. "Continue your discussion of your purpose for the restaurant."

Mr. James responded. "Martin and Ray have spent the most time thinking about this. Martin, since this is your idea, please share your vision with Miss Bright. And Ray, please feel free to share your ideas."

`Martin, looking at each member at the table, turned his full attention to Bonnie Bright. "I'm most looking for ways we engage all the people that work at or use Supreme Foods. As I thought this through, I questioned, ' Do our employees know the foods they create or how the general public responds to what they have created? 'They do eat lunch, dinner or have snacks and coffee during a 'break' time. Having them together for meals contributes to a feeling of family. Groups function better when members know each other and trust each other. Hopefully, productivity is increased when individuals care about each other and the work they do."

Ray added. "I've been impressed with the history of the company. Very early in my relationship with the company, I've learned the founder, Grandmother James, insisted on quality. When I visited the home in which she raised her large family and prepared food for her neighbors, I saw a simple, very functional setting. Many of her cooking items still hang in place in her kitchen. I envision a replication of simple, antique-like setting. Perhaps seeing copies of cooking equipment on the walls of the restaurant leading to the kitchen with a large painting of Grandmother James."

Jimmy James interrupted, "What a beautiful idea! I remember well the sights and smell of her kitchen!"

Martin picked up the conversation. "Finding ways of helping employees become invested in the company, I believe, will create a more supportive environment for workers. If employees enjoy the foods they help prepare, I believe they will begin to suggest ways of increasing the quality of the foods. I've even thought that if workers make suggestions for new products or ways of increasing the effective use of the foods, they might be awarded with shares in the company's stock. This might end up with employees having a greater investment in the company, giving them a desire to express themselves creatively. Having ownership in something promotes commitment. My observation in many companies is that when the greatest amount of money goes to a few there is less feeling of desire to produce quality in the production. Control is always less effective than invitations to participation."

"Wow! How brilliant an idea, Martin!" Leland exclaimed. "Great Grandmother James would have been excited about such an idea, at least from what I've learned from stories I've heard about her!"

"I think you're very right, Leland. I'm really getting a picture of what I think everyone is moving toward," said Bonnie. "You may not be only creating great quality products, but you may be giving direction to some productive ways of increasing administration and the distribution of wealth! I believe I have the beginning of a vision for the restaurant. It may be a setting with a sense of history. I think I'm ready to begin designing your restaurant. If I have questions, with whom should I discuss them?"

"Martin and Ray. They will bring the questions and their responses to us. We are becoming a very collaborative unit which I feel is good for Supreme Foods! Thank you, Ms Bright, for a very helpful session," responded Leland. "I've gotten the clue from my father that we need to get back to our office to keep things running."

They quickly left the restaurant, got in Bonnie's car and made their way back to Supreme Foods.

They thanked Ms Bright and entered the administration offices.

As they passed through the suite offices, the secretary greeted them and then directed her comments to Martin. "A Miss Gladys Smith from Pierce called asking you to call her back, today if possible."

"Now, what can that be about?" thought Martin. "What is urgent that I need to call her today" Martin spoke to the secretary. "Thank you. I hope I have her telephone number."

"I have her number on the note. Is she a friend of yours?'

"One might say so. She was once my wife."

Chapter 26

A Reunion: New Beginnings

Martin picked up the telephone note, and entering his office, anxiously anticipated the call.. What is she wanting? Is there something not yet resolved? Was he not fully forgiven? He got up out of his chair and paced the room attempting to assemble his courage to make the call. He thought, "Why do I always expect the worst? What can the call be about?"

He finally tensed his muscles and sat before his phone. He picked up the note and began dialing her cell phone number. "She's probably at the library working her magic with the children!" He smiled at the thought of watching her invite the children into their stories. He heard the ringing: one, two, three, four, five. The ringing stopped. Someone has picked up the phone.

"Hello". The voice was unfamiliar. "This is the Gladys Smith residence. Would you like to talk with Gladys? Wait a moment. She's packing." He could hear to sound of the phone being placed on the stand.

"This is Gladys Smith. May I help you?

"I trust you remember my voice? This is Martin. I was out at lunch when you called my office. My secretary said you had called and that I was to call back today? Is there something wrong? Something you need me to do?"

"My friend and I are coming to Bloomfield and we are anxious to talk with you. We are leaving tomorrow morning early and should be in Bloomfield by noon. May we meet you at your office, your apartment or at a hotel? By the way, that was one of Franklin's daughters on the phone. She is here helping me pack."

"Don't come to my apartment. It's terrible. I went there to hide after our divorce. I felt I was such a loser. I wanted to hide from life. I'll share more when we meet. Could we meet at the church on the other side of the park? I want you to meet Dr. Beatrice Bonner, my very special friend who counseled me to meet with you and has been with me in the events that followed. She is a psychologist and an ordained minister. Then we can go to the little 'hole-in-the-wall' restaurant nearby. The food is wonderful and the service is great. Many things in my entering life again happened there. The park is a meeting place in that part of Bloomfield."

"Sounds like a plan! See you tomorrow at about 10:30!" And his telephone went dead.

Martin stopped by Leland's office to say he would like me to meet with his father and him. Leland picked up at phone and called his father. "Martin would like to ask something of us. Are you available now?" He couldn't hear the reply but from the facial response knew they were on the way to the next door.

Mr. James questioned, "Did you want to share something or need something?"

"Yes and yes! When we returned from lunch I had a call from my former wife asking that I call her today. I doubt that you know what has taken place since Dr. Bonner has opened me to life. Of all the other things, I give her credit for orchestrating an invitation for me to see Gladys, my former wife, and to receive some resolution to some unfinished matters. It was a moment of grace. With deep anxiety I went to Pierce, Ohio, where Gladys and I first met and where we married. She had returned and took back her maiden name. I found her working with children in the public library. I told her I would like to take her to a nice restaurant for dinner so we could talk. She replied that there are no nice restaurants in Pierce

137

but she was doing a stew for her friend Franklin Pierce, a descendent of the founders of the village. He is the chair of the library board. His wife recently died leaving him with young children. Gladys began helping the family with learning to cope with their grief and the work about the house. It had developed into a very deep relationship. Franklin invited her to move in with him. She refused until his children accepted her. She and Franklin are coming tomorrow to talk with me, arriving at about 10:30. We plan to meet in Dr. Bonner's office at your church. I don't know the purpose of the visit, but I would like the time to meet with them. I want them to know Beatrice."

"By all means do go. While we don't know the full history of events, we do know how important it is to confirm relationships."

"Thank you. I know when I asked forgiveness for my earlier behavior, Gladys and I embraced and with tears found newness for our lives, a reconciliation." He thanked them returning to his office and attempting to work. He was so filled with anxiousness that his efforts at work were unlikely. While it was not time to end the day, Martin picked some papers to be reviewed should he feel like working.

The day and the night wore on with little rest available. Was not their relationship in Pierce completed? What more would she want from him? Why did he anticipate the unsettling nature of their previous relationship? The anticipated meeting was fully in his thoughts. The uneasiness continued until darkness came and the slit in the shade cast the light from the streetlight on the wall by his bed. He turned back the bedding, undressed to his shorts and laid his head on the pillow. Turning over, he pulled the covers over his head and began his heavy sleep breathing

It was 4:00 A.M. when Martin opened an eye and glanced at the clock. "Only 4:00 A.M.? Will this night never end? Why am I so anxious concerning Gladys' visit?"

He turned over, drew the covers back up over his head, and because of such a restless night, was soon back in dreamland. It was eight o'clock when he awakened. Ray had quietly visited the bathroom, and eaten his bowl of cornflakes. Even the crunch of the cereal didn't awaken Martin. Ray was long gone. As a matter of fact Martin didn't hear his coming in. What time did he come home? Was it another of those special painting sessions?

"Good grief! Now I've done it! I want to get to the park just in case Beatrice shows up. I need to warn her of what is about to happen," He kicked off the covers, slipped out of bed, rushed to the bathroom, then quickly dressed for the day. Foregoing breakfast, he hurried down the steps and found his place on his bench in the park. So caught up in his thoughts for the day, he didn't hear the birds singing or the laughter of children at play.

"Well, Genius, what great thought invade this space?"

Martin was so deep in his thoughts that he failed to notice that Beatrice had quietly rolled in her chair close to where Martin was sitting. "A penny for your thoughts!" she continued.

"Am I glad to see you! Yesterday I received a call from Gladys. She and Franklin are coming to see me. They didn't share with me what the visit was about. I can't imagine the reason for the trip. I hope nothing is wrong. I thought the meeting with them in Pierce resolved the problems that we once had. Why do I expect some problem? What's going on in my thick head?"

"Think of something positive, that they are coming for a positive experience growing from your relationship on your trip to Pierce."

"I do want them to meet and know you. I invited them to meet at your church and then we'll go to our favorite restaurant for lunch and conversation. I'm sorry for setting that up without consulting with you. Forgive me. Everything was so unexpected that I had to think fast. If that isn't okay I would plan to meet them and find another place where we could talk."

"That's fine. I was so moved by your story of your meeting them in Pierce and the richness of forgiveness, that I look forward to meeting them. They must be very special people. Shall we head back to the church to be ready for their arrival? If you'd like you could push me back to the church"

"And we don't even have a potential cloudburst! Want to go fast this time, too?" They both chuckled remembering the hilarious first meeting when they felt like two young kids playing a game, racing as fast as they could go to beat the storm. As they raced forward, Martin thought of all the things that had happened in his life because of that initial meeting. As they entered the church he looked at his watch aware that in a little more than a half hour, Gladys and Franklin would arrive.

Chapter 27

The Engagement

Once inside the church and in Beatrice's office, time seemed to race on. At ten fifteen, Martin began to pace back and forth in her office. His thoughts unexpressed were very present with him. What is the purpose of their visit? How would he begin the conversation?

Beatrice watched the drama being played out. There were many other times when she had worked with people, when such strong anxieties existed, and how often they had little to do with what occurred.

Suddenly, Beatrice's office phone rang. He could hear the secretary say, "There's a Miss Smith and a Mr. Pierce hear to meet with Mr. Roberts!"

Martin, for a moment, felt the whole world had stopped moving. He stood speechless as he went to the door of the office. Opening the door, he looked at Gladys without a word. Suddenly Gladys opened her arms and they embraced.

Gladys said, "And this must be Dr. Bonner?"

"It's Beatrice to you."

Gladys continued to direct the conversation and the activities. "Beatrice, meet my very special friend Franklin Pierce."

Franklin went to Beatrice, bending down to embrace her. He then turned to Martin and with outstretched arms embraced him.

All the while Gladys had given her attention to Beatrice as they embraced.

Gladys continued to prompt the conversation."When Martin came to Pierce to find me, it became a very special time. What I have learned from villagers, he went with real intent to find me. They directed him to the public library where I was working with children and their learning the story of "Charlotte's Web" by E.B. White. When he entered the room where I was reading and working with children, I looked up and saw him. It was Martin alright, but there was something very different about him. I was caught by surprise by whatever there was that didn't feel like the Martin I had known. I kept stealing a glance as we continued our work with the students, hoping to discover what was different. His eyes literally danced as he watched the children dramatize parts of the story. The restless part I had known was now wonderfully patient. He seemed very interested in what the children were discovering about this very special story. Then he said that he wanted to take me to a very nice restaurant so that we might talk. I told him there were no nice restaurants in this tiny village of Pierce, but that I was cooking a stew and that Franklin was coming for dinner. Would he like to join us."

"I'm addicted to Gladys' stew. Once you've tasted it no other stew can match it!"

"The whole dinner hour was a most wonderful experience. It was a real joy. There was no feeling of having to get on with it. Time was to be available for that which we were searching for, that getting to know Franklin was a priority."

"With a stomach filled with Gladys' stew, what more could one expect?"

"We were so surprised when Martin confessed his feelings of not being present to my grief when our son Jack was killed. I almost lost it. Then when he asked for my forgiveness I did lose it. With tears caressing my cheeks I got up and went to him to embrace him. He removed a clean handkerchief from his pocket to dry my tears. I looked at him to see tears on his face. I gave him back his handkerchief and our tears came together in that piece of cloth."

"That handkerchief has not been touched since that moment of forgiveness," Martin volunteered. "I'm so fully aware of the many changes in my life. Most of them are due to the love and caring of Beatrice as we have gotten to more fully know each other. As we came together in the park across the street from my one room apartment, it was she who invited me back to life. It is she who invited me to look deeply into those things that have denied me life. It had been her invitation to my giving of myself to others that has resulted in what you wondered about as you've noted a change in how I face life."

Beatrice added, "One can create an invitation, but it is the result of the individual wanting to change, that creates the change. It is the forgiveness of others or of oneself that makes renewal possible. All that you both have talked about could not have happened had you not deeply within yourselves cared enough to bring about these changes."

"Is anyone else as hungry as I? Martin, didn't you say something about a very special little restaurant nearby?" Franklin was interested in becoming a part of what was taking place.

Gladys continued, "I understand it is within walking distance and it's probably easier to walk the wheelchair that to get in a car for that short a distance. It is important that we drive to the restaurant. We have a gift in the car for Martin. Tell me again just where the restaurant is!"

Beatrice volunteered, "It's less than a block from the church. You'll recognize it for an artist is doing pictures of customers from his "studio" in the front window."

With little more direction, everyone got up and left Beatrice's office and the church. A kind of calm had come over Martin as he reflected on the affirmation and caring expressed when they all came together. He relished the feelings that he was having. What a joy it has been.

When they arrived at the restaurant, Ray Wynn was busy creating a picture of a client. He interrupted his drawing to meet the new people in the group. He was also aware of the peacefulness he saw in Martin, being very aware of the anxiety he was having, not knowing the purpose for Gladys and Franklin's visit to Bloomfield. The party was seated. Ray smiled when he saw his gorgeous lover being assigned to the table. She quickly distributed menus and served glasses of water.

"And what would you like to drink?" Each gave their choice and they were quietly served. One by one they placed their order.

When they had finished ordering Franklin said, "Excuse me. I have something in my car to bring in! With that, he left the table and the restaurant. Everyone began to question what it was to be shared. Within a very short time, he came through the door carrying an object.

Martin turned around to see the large red fire truck. With tears welling in his eyes, he tried to hide his response.

"Oh, my God, the fire truck I gave Jack for his fifth birthday!" he exclaimed as he turned his head that others could not see the tears beginning to gather in his eyes.

Gladys spoke softly to Martin, "It's yours! I want you to have it!"

Martin thrust his hand covering his face as he began to sob. Bernice, seated beside him, put her arms around his shoulders as if to cradle him. Gladys got up from her chair on the other side of the table and with tears came to Martin to share in a long unexpressed grief. Franklin, seeing what was happening, reached in his rear pocket retrieving a clean handkerchief, putting it in Gladys' hand. Beatrice began crying, feeling the pain Martin was experiencing at long last. Soon the handkerchief held the tears of three people caught in a love that one could not have predicted. Franklin also became a part of this most intimate event.

Ray stopped painting for his caring. Even though he did not know some of the people, he had been profoundly affected by members of the group. Perhaps someday he might reflect on this most unusual event and it would find its way to a canvas. He spotted his love and motioned to delay the serving of the food.

Beatrice, with her tear-soaked eyes, looked across Martin to Gladys. As their eyes met, they seemed to say, "Did Martin ever fully grieve the death of his son? Did they not share together in that grief? While painful, but in a way, that fire truck has become a beautiful gift. Gladys and Martin have shared at a depth they had never before known. I never heard him talk about his son, but only that he was not there for Gladys' grieving. Would his guilt, in not being fully present to his son, deny his grief?"

For quite a time nothing happened. It was as if the whole world could witness the true power of love, a grace not expected or knowingly planned. They could be a part of life and the presence of grace, which most often comes as a surprise; all must be open to understanding its presence and its power.

It was Gladys who continued the opening. "Martin, Jack truly loved you. He wanted so much to become your true son, so that there would be times to be together and share your lives. When he died in the accident, I moved into his room, to remind me of him, to share a bit of him. That fire truck was in the room. When I finally stopped crying, I saw the fire truck and in touching it, rolling it across the floor, I fully remembered those joyous days in his life. It assisted me in remembering. I want you to know the joy we once found in sharing a son!"

Martin raised his head, and turning to Gladys with his red, tear-soaked eyes, reached out and embraced her in a kind of love he had seldom known before. Almost everyone in the restaurant retrieved their napkins to dab the tears resulting from the beauty of the moment.

Almost in unison, there was a sigh, audible to all as if one of life's greatest events had nearly come to an end, and that everything was coming out as Life intended.

The restaurant came alive. Chefs from the kitchen, who had come to witness the event, returned to the sound of pots and pans. Waiters and waitresses picked up their pitchers and trays to replenish water glasses and to begin bringing food the tables. Dotty made her way to the table, and in an uncustomary way, reached out to

Gladys and Martin in a quick embrace.

Ray sat at an empty table deep in thought of what he had just witnessed. Did this have something to do with the conversation he and Dotty had one night during the nude painting session? What is the source of love? How can we find it in the midst of our struggles? So many questions to think about. And how does one translate that to paint and a canvas?

Gladys again spoke to those at the table, as they began their salads. "Martin, when you called, you heard the voice of one of Franklin's daughters, who was at my apartment helping us pack for the trip today. After a time of their grieving and my chance to serve them, they wanted their father to experience love in his life. They came to me and began calling me "Mother." Like the sigh we just heard here, Franklin and I had our sigh. We plan to be married very soon. I have no family except the family I've found today. We would like you and Beatrice to be involved in our wedding! Could you come to Pierce and participate? I would like Beatrice to conduct our wedding vows. Since you are now a part of my family I would like you to accompany me down the aisle."

There was an audible sound of surprise as those within earshot turned to watch what would happen next.

Beatrice continued. "I would love to share in your marriage. Today I witnessed the power of love, a forgiveness and giveness not often experienced. If Martin is willing, count me in."

It was Martin's time. "Love insists on finding its own way. As I have just discovered, it come in packages of its own choosing. If that is your request, I will be there."

Chapter 28

The Wedding

Two weeks seemed to rush by. Everyone was pressed into service. Beatrice dusted off the book with the wedding vows. Martin thought deeply about what he would say and do when he accompanied Gladys down the aisle. Gladys arranged with the local church for decorations to adorn the space. There would be a rehearsal to be conducted, and housing for out of town guests, since there were so few motels and no hotels in Pierce. And since there were no nice restaurants in Pierce, would she have to prepare a wedding luncheon or dinner, or would some neighbor assist? The Franklin children wanted to be fully involved. Gladys would need to arrange tasks for them to make sure they had ownership in the event. While in one sense time flew by, in another sense, how would they get everything done in time?

Beatrice had a conference with Gladys and Franklin, even though both had gone through a marriage before. It seemed more to offer a blessing than for an awareness of their commitments. How she would move in her wheelchair was practiced. Gladys' neighbors planned and created a lovely reception for the bride and groom and their guests to follow the wedding. All seemed ready.

Even Martin was excited for the event, so different from his marriage with Gladys. In their youthful passion and the seeming need for what they thought was intimacy, Gladys had gotten pregnant. Their marriage was a hurried trip to the justice of peace. There was no reception. No celebration! Just meet the expected social norms! He gathered together a couple of items to share in the ceremony.

At last the anticipated day came. The Franklin children got up early, prepared breakfast for their father, did the dishes, and helped each other dress for the wedding. Everything had to be just perfect.

The whole village of Pierce was dressed for the occasion. It would be a high point for the whole village.

Martin had gotten up early, gulped down his breakfast, and dressed in his Sunday best. He grabbed the one item to be shared and drove to Beatrice's apartment to take her to Pierce with him. She was dressed in a formal black skirt and jacket, which would make it easier for her to manage her braces, should that be required. She was waiting at the main door to her apartment building. Martin smiled in delight upon seeing her. He parked the car and hurriedly raced to greet her. She smiled as her bent over to kiss her.

He pushed her wheel chair to his car and assisted her in standing as she adjusted her braces. With tenderness, he helped her into the passenger seat. He folded the wheelchair and placed it in the trunk of his car. It all seemed so natural and easy to do, having shared their travels more often.

The trip to Pierce was an exciting time. Every experience with Beatrice was becoming increasingly important. Just being with her brought Martin great joy. Conversations were special. There would be moments when the rush of words seemed to stack on each other's thoughts. Then there were moments when silence prevailed. What was happening in that silence? What were they thinking? Was it about what was to take place in a very short time? Or was it about their own relationship, how they met and the excitement of discovering life anew? How the experience of living seemed to become greater every moment they had together?

In no time they were in Pierce. In this small village with only one church, it was not difficult to find it. Martin drove to a spot where it would be easy to assist Beatrice in getting back into her wheelchair. That had become well-practiced for them. It took no time until they were ready to enter the church. Martin pushed the wheelchair to the entrance of the church.

Gladys had arrived just prior to Martin and Beatrice's arrival. She had not yet entered the church. Seeing them, she picked up the hem of her white formal gown and moved to them. She bent over to kiss Beatrice and hug her. She smiled warmly at Martin. Not a word was said. Words would have disturbed the tenderness of the moment. She entered the church and stood alone at the back of the church.

Martin pushed Beatrice to the area in front of the altar before returning to stand with Gladys. Not a word was said.

Franklin, in his excitement for the day, had arrived earlier and was remaining in a room at the front of the church. Two of his sons were with him. His daughters made their way to the area where Gladys and Martin stood. When they arrived, they went to Gladys and planted a kiss on her cheek. Not a word was said. Words were not necessary to express their feelings.

The music teacher in the local high school, Virginia Pierce, was the best musician in the village and the person who provided the music for the church. She was a relative of Franklin. She began a short recital to begin the service as villagers made their way to the pews. The smell of food and coffee brewing in the basement made its way to the sanctuary. Everyone settled in, ready to witness the marriage.

Martin reached in his pocket and withdrew a handkerchief. "I'd like you to have this piece of cloth. It's the handkerchief that Franklin gave to you when you gave Jack's fire truck to me, and in my grief I dissolved in tears. Your tears and those of Beatrice were combined in it as both of you came together to support me. Please accept it with my love."

She took the handkerchief and tucked it under the bracelet she was wearing. They looked down the aisle and saw that Beatrice had taken her place, turning her wheelchair around to face the congregation and the marriage party. Franklin and his two sons took their place and beamed with joy. The congregation stood as Gladys and Martin made their way down the aisle.

The music stopped and Dr. Bonner began the ceremony with, "Who gives this woman in marriage?"

Martin spoke with strength and affirmation, "It is I, Martin Roberts, her former husband, forgiven, and now her spiritual, soul brother." And with that, he reached down, taking Franklin's hand and placing it with Gladys' hand. Then he held them together by surrounding their clasp with his own. For a brief moment, he held the joining of their hands. Martin returned to a seat with the congregation.

Beatrice was touched by the beauty of the moment. Her eyes glistened with a tear. Before continuing with the ritual, she announced her observation. "I must share what I saw as Martin gave Gladys in the marriage. Following his statement, he reached down, taking Franklin's hand and placing it with Gladys' hand. Then he surrounded their hands with his own clasp, demonstrating a tenderness seldom seen in a moment such as this. Knowing their histories, I was moved to tears." A brief moment of silence followed as she regained her composure and the congregation had time to reflect on what she had just shared. She then continued the ritual, ending with, "It is with joy that I introduce you to Mr. and Mrs. Franklin Pierce."

Martin rose from his seat and went to Beatrice, bending down to embrace her. Then, to their surprise, the newly-wedded couple bent down, and the four embraced to share the love that was fully present. Members of the congregation, deeply moved by this scene of love, found themselves reaching out to each other.

After a brief moment, it was Gladys that moved the action forward. With a strong voice she began, "Food for soul is wonderful, and I thank you. Food for the body is wonderful, too. I think I smell coffee. Please follow my new, beautiful daughters to the aroma!" And with that, there were no more instructions. They found their way to the cakes, pies and elegant finger foods.

An amazing response happened over coffee and tidbits. They

shared their feelings of the beauty they experienced in the ceremony. This, in turn, spawned other stories of those beautiful moments that occurred in a graceful way at their own marriages or other ceremonies they had attended. Was it the presence of total forgiveness and the affirmation for life that prompted their responses? Or was there something about the honest openness that is so seldom seen? And they reflected on what they experienced. They, without uttering their comments, began to ask about what keeps them from being present to such grace?

Almost everyone in Pierce was at the wedding. They all warmly greeted the wedding couple. Many of the men, with a sense of embarrassment and hesitation, gave Gladys a kiss on her cheek. Martin and Beatrice stood alone at one side. Often, individuals would glance at Martin and Beatrice, but seemingly not knowing quite how to address them, avoided coming near them. Divorces in Pierce almost never happened. And then to see the couple together was even more unusual.

It was the three Franklin daughters who came rushing up to Beatrice and Martin, throwing their arms about each of them and then, almost in unison, said, "Thank you for the beautiful gift you've given our family. Father is deeply in love with Gladys and we children are most happy with Gladys as our new mother."

It is interesting how children lead. Their affirmation of Beatrice and Martin was the permission needed for others to follow. One by one, many came to express their joy for the love that was engendered during the wedding. While they could not find the words to share their ideas, the action spoke loudly of the power of forgiveness. A kind of wholeness in relationships was present.

An extra cup of coffee and a small piece of the three-tiered wedding cake brought the event to a close. Martin pushed Beatrice's wheelchair to his car and helped her into her seat. Folding the wheelchair and placing it in the trunk, they were soon on their way back to Bloomfield. Little was said, as they both seemed to sense the significance of the wedding and the sequences of the events that led to what had just happened. Martin was remembering how he had tried to hide from life, but that it is in the midst of a storm that he experienced the grace that led him to Beatrice and the renewal of his life.

As they drew up to the front of Beatricc's apartment building, Martin turned off the motor, then leaning over, folded his arms about her and kissed her. "Thank you for all the gifts you have given me. And thank God for rain storms!" He paused for a moment as if he had just tasted a most delicious dessert and he wanted to hold it in his memory. He turned to get out of the car, secure her wheelchair, assist her in getting back into her chair, and push her to her apartment suite.

Beatrice looked into Martin's eyes and read his thoughts. "Please come in. I need to share with you what I've been thinking about."

Martin took her keys, and opening the door, pushed her into the room. His actions were rather obvious. His thoughts were unspoken, "Do I dare share with her what is most deeply etched in my mind? Certainly she must know how deeply I have grown to love her. I don't want anything to disrupt the strong feeling of love and caring I have for her."

Beatrice felt his responses fully. She began, "Martin, the gifts you gave through your actions was so powerful. Never have I felt such caring as you showed at the wedding. It was all I could do to stop the tears. I have never felt such love in my whole life. Your caring for Gladys and Franklin was overwhelming. That is the kind of love I feel for you. I don't want anything to come in the way of our developing love. Please stay with me tonight. I want to know you, everything about you. I was once loved back to life after polio. Now I am loved to life by love itself." She pulled Martin down to her and kissed him strongly on his lips, holding the kiss for what seemed to be for Martin intended for an eternity.

Martin could not find words to express his feelings. How could she know what was really in my thoughts? When two people are so deeply in love, do they always know the depth of their being? How wonderful to open oneself to bare their very souls! But then he began thinking of details connecting with staying the night.

Beatrice replied, "Don't worry about your car. Let it stay there for the night. And you're probably worrying about other things. Pajamas? Who needs them? "Nothing more was said as he pushed her wheelchair to her bedroom, and with tenderness, helped her to the bed. He asked her to direct his removing of her braces. Unlocking her braces, he removed them. Item by item, her clothing was taken from her, revealing a beautiful body waiting to be found.

He bent over her, kissing her warmly and passionately.

Beatrice reached up, untied his tie, unbuttoned his shirt, and waited until he had removed his shoes and socks, and his pants, and crawled into bed beside her. Little more needed to be said as they wrapped their arms about each other. Martin reached up and turned off the light.

Chapter 29

Back at Work

Martin awakened early, as was his practice. He dressed quietly and made his way to the kitchen to prepare a breakfast for Beatrice. Having never been in the apartment, since he did not know how she organized things for her convenience, he explored the cupboard to find breakfast makings, trying to be quiet lest he awaken her.

"Hey, you! Breakfast is a woman's job!" she said as she came wheeling in, fully dressed.

"Not when you're being taken out for breakfast at our favorite 'hole in the wall' restaurant before dropping you off at the church. Get yourself in gear, for I'm hungry."

"No rain storm needed to get things started today!" Martin exclaimed, as he directed their energies toward the restaurant.

Dotty saw them coming and raced to the door to open it for their entrance. "One doesn't have to dress formally for breakfast at this restaurant!" she said, looking at them with a questioning look. "Come in, I'm sure we have something left to feed two hungry people." She seated them at a table near the front where Ray did much of art work in the window. .

"I'm expecting Ray to pop in any minute. What would you like to drink? Coffee? Tea? What will it be?" she said as she placed glasses of water at each of their places. "Oh, here comes Ray now!"

She set her tray, her pad, and her pencil at an empty table, and, opening her arms, greeted Ray with a kiss. "Look who's joined us for breakfast, love! And dressed to impress us!"

"Hmm, now I know why no one slept in your bed last night. Can you explain what happened?" Ray asked.

We were at a wedding," Martin added.

"The two of you?"

"Yes."

"The two of you got married?"

"No! But that's a great idea. We'll think that over! We drove to Pierce for Gladys' wedding with Franklin Pierce. We got back to Bloomfield quite late."

"And you were so tired that you chose to sleep elsewhere?" Ray questioned with a glint in his eye. Back in his "studio," he studied the couple intently. "Dotty, come here. Are these the same people we have known before? As an artist, I search for that something in others that reveals their souls. Is that what I'm seeing? Has something awakened their souls? Get me my camera. I don't want to lose this picture!" Dotty brought him his camera, and Ray snapped several pictures as Martin and Beatrice studied the menu and snuck a knowing glance to each other. Even they were aware of that something was different in their lives.

Beatrice, anxious to redirect the conversation, said, "I'd like your ham and cheese omelet, two eggs, not three, and no toast. I think I'd like a small glass of orange juice."

Martin thought, "She knows how to keep us focused and moving ahead. I'm amazed at her means of inviting others to her sense of wholeness. Now look at me, here I am beginning to think in her language."

"Make that two poached eggs, two strips of bacon and dry rye toast," Martin volunteered. "Be careful of what you do with those pictures, Ray. I might have to throw you out of the apartment!"

"Hmmm! Interesting! Are you planning to spend much time there? I could probably find another roommate! Sorry, Beatrice, I just like what I'm seeing!" Ray picked up his smock and paint brushes and getting a fresh canvas, began sketching a new painting that has captured his interests.

It didn't take long to do a couple of eggs, toast, ham or bacon. Martin paid the bill and leaving a generous tip, began their trip back to Beatrice's office, and then on his own way to the Supreme Food Products offices.

As he pulled into the parking lot, he was surprised to see a large area already blocked off and workmen beginning to prepare the area for the new addition of the restaurant. Leland stood at one side, complete with sunglasses and a cap to shade his head. Martin headed directly to Leland. "You don't waste any time in getting things started. I'm gone a couple of days and look at what's going on. But then that's a James tradition. Is your father here?"

"You don't have to dress so formally just to work here," Leland countered. Dad has gone out to his grandmother's place. The designs Ray has planned for this restaurant, to give the sense of her home where Supreme Foods got its start, has stirred his imagination. And your proposal that we create a living museum of life in the early twentieth century on her farm has captured his thinking. And why the formal dress?"

"Beatrice and I went to Pierce to participate in the wedding of Gladys and Franklin Pierce. I didn't get home in time to change," Martin said, turning his face away to avoid showing his feelings and perhaps revealing what really happened.

Leland continued, "I'm not sure, for Dad has not talked about it, but I sometimes feel he should get out of the demands of managing the company. First, he named himself chairman of the board, making me president. He often talks about your idea of the living museum on my great-grandmother's property. Don't be surprised if he moves out there and creates the museum."

"I probably need to go back to my apartment and change my clothes, otherwise I'll have explaining to do all day."

In the days to follow, the work progressed quickly in the creation of the construction. Leland visited with Lily Wong's Cooking

School, to prepare her young chefs to bring the restaurant to life. When the construction was completed Ray decorated the walls and set the dining area to reflect Grandmother James' spirit.

Everything advanced as planned. The young chefs did their very best. Employees and visitors to the restaurant were high in their praise. Employees shared their ideas and were awarded shares in the company. Visitors shared their favorite family recipes, and when it resulted in new products for the company, they, too, were given shares in the company.

Supreme Foods was experiencing significant growth. Everyone looked to Martin for his leadership.

Chapter 30

The Love Feast

On February first, Martin's phone rang. Rushing to it, he picked it up and said, "Hello."

"Martin, this is Beatrice."

"Of course I recognize your voice."

"Save dinner for Valentine Day. I booked a special room for our dinner, a special love feast."

"I think that's my responsibility to take you to dinner."

"All detail are set. I've reserved a room at the Marley Hotel. Would it be okay to invite your roommate and his girl friend to join us?"

"That would be fine. They're such a fine couple. Ray is spending more time with her. I'm impressed with their devotion to each other. That's a go! What time have you set for our intimate dinner? May I pick you up a half hour before the dinner time to make sure we can get a parking place convenient for you to your get into the hotel?"

"Sounds like a good plan to me! Would you like to come to my apartment for dinner this evening? I'll rustle up something to keep us going. Bye!" With that, she ended their conversation.

Beatrice said little more about her planned love feast. When Martin asked Ray about the event, Ray was tight-lipped, and feigned ignorance about the dinner.

"Must be some common event," Martin thought, since so little more was said. "I suppose I'll do as she wants. She always does things for the good of our relationship!"

On February thirteenth, Beatrice called Martin to arrange her pick-up. "Our little love feast is scheduled for seven. Would you pick me up at six thirty? I've reserved a parking space to accommodate my entry into the hotel. The hotel has been very helpful." With no more than that, she hung up the phone. Martin thought it made good sense. Beatrice thinks of everything.

Martin picked up a beautiful corsage of red roses for Beatrice and a white carnation for the lapel of his suit. "I want to make this very special for my love." He stopped at the jewelry shop for one more purchase. "This night will be very special!"

The day seemed to drag on at work. He couldn't get involved in his work for thinking of the events at their dinner. It also seemed strange that he saw very few of the people at the company. He understood Leland's absence, for he'd gotten very involved with the restaurant they had created. Mr. James hadn't even come to his office. Even the secretary was busy and unavailable. But then, none of that mattered as he thought of what he would be doing at their little love feast Beatrice had planned at the Marley.

At last, the work day had ended. Martin took no work with him. The night would be reserved for things that were most important.

By five the next day, he had dressed in his best suit and fastened the white carnation to his lapel.

Ray came rushing in and hit the shower. Feeling fresh and excited, he dressed for the evening. "I hope you don't mind, Beatrice invited Dotty and me to join you two for the love feast. That's most proper, for I've asked Dotty to be my bride."

Martin had learned to trust Beatrice's judgment. "I'm pleased, Ray. I've watched love grow deeply in your relationship. That will be another celebration. We'll be celebrating tonight. Celebrations are the frosting on the cake! I know it's early, but I don't want to be late for my date with Beatrice!" He pulled his topcoat about him, slipped his special purchase in his suit pocket, picked up the red rose corsage from the refrigerator, then made his way down the steps to his car. Sitting in his car, he began thinking just how he would propose to Beatrice. He practiced many different phrases, wanting even the words he used to be special. He, having practiced, had decided just how he would do it. He'd get down on his knee, and, taking her hand, would slip the ring on her finger and say, "I love you with my whole life. Will you marry me?" He looked at his watch. If he didn't drive too fast, he'd get there just in time to go to her apartment and push he chair to car awaiting them.

Martin made his way to her apartment. He rang the door bell, anxiously waiting to see her. When she opened the door, he saw her excitedly awaiting him. She was dressed in a beautiful soft blue suit, with a slightly darker blue scarf about her neck. She was radiant. She reached out for his hand, and drawing him down to her, kissed him in a way that caused him to think, "Please, God, don't let this ever end!"

He reached for her coat, carefully placed on a nearby chair, and wrapped it about her. They began their journey to the Marley.

Just as she had planned, there was a young man ready to take his car and park it for him. He unlocked the trunk and went around to retrieve her chair. Another young man was ahead of him, and already had the chair out of the trunk, ready for her transfer to the chair.

Martin looked about him. The parking lot was filled. "Must be something important going on at the hotel this evening. I can't remember seeing so many cars here before!"

"You're probably right. Maybe they're having a love feast of their own, too!" Beatrice replied.

Ray Wynn and Dotty had arrived just ahead of them. Ray carried a rather large object with him. "Martin, let me catch the door for you. Maybe I can help you to our dining room." Juggling the package in one hand, he moved to open the door, but a doorman opened it, greeting them all as Martin pushed Beatrice into the lobby.

"Let's go down the hallway over at our left," Beatrice volunteered.

"But that's the way to the ball rooms and the large dining area."

"We have to go through one of those rooms to get to where we're to have our love feast dinner. It is all planned so just go on!"

They moved on. Ray came rushing up from behind them. "Wait, I'll get the door!" He opened the door, standing in front of them so Martin could not see inside the room.

As he entered the room, he stopped, catching his breath, he stood there speechless. In front of him were a crowd of people fully known to him. Mr. James and Leland were at a head table. Two empty seats were at the center and two at one side. "Welcome, Martin, to a Love Feast in your honor."

Tears glistened in his eyes as he struggled to hold back from crying. Two young men came, and pushing Beatrice to the front of the room, invited him to follow them to the head table. On the way down the aisle, Gladys and Franklin Pierce stepped into the aisle to embrace him. Many others along the aisle reached out to shake his hand. When they reached the head table, two young men reached down, lifted Beatrice from her chair, and carried her to one of the empty seats at the center. Another young waiter ushered Martin to his seat at the very center of the table.

It was then that Mr. James stood, and addressing Martin that all might hear, said, "Martin, I present you the keys to Supreme Foods." He handed the keys to Martin. "Leland and I have marveled at the manner in which you have empowered all the people in our company. Your vision of what is possible has brought our company to a very distinguishing level. Your suggestions have resulted in our employees being more than just workers and becoming engaged to a sense of ownership. Your vision of their unique contributions, having given greater depth and breadth to the company, has given them shares in the company, and results in their greater commitment.

"Your influence has been more that what grows within the company, but how our company serves the greater community. When you and Ray visited my grandmother's home to develop of feeling of her life for the restaurant at the company, and you proposed that we make her homestead into a living museum of what life was like early in this century, I was moved, so moved that I am moving back to the homestead where we will restore her one hundred sixty acres to what it was like when she lived there. Your vision was significant as we attempt to remind ourselves of our heritage.

"I can imagine school children coming to the farm to see cows being milked by hand, milk being processed into cheese, as my grandmother did it, and maybe even giving students the opportunity to use the wooden tub in which she stomped the cream into butter. There seems to be no end to your visions.

"Because I wish to develop this living museum and deciding to move there to assure its happening, I'm retiring as chairman of the board, making Leland the chair, and we've decided to invite you to the presidency of Supreme Food Products."

The entire group stood with loud applause, in affirmation, for each had their own stories of how he had empowered each of them.

Martin stood, accepting the symbol of the keys, fighting back tears, but not knowing what to say, "What a wonderful gift. I need a few minutes to gather my thoughts. Anyway, you all came here for dinner, and then I will share my journey to this moment in our time. Thank you Leland and Mr. James."

Quickly and quietly the waiters came, refilling water glasses, then offering a choice of white and red wine. They brought a variety of house dressings for the salads and fresh ground pepper for their choices. Shortly thereafter, they entered with a small steak and Lake Erie pike, twice-baked potatoes, and asparagus served with a peanut sauce. In the end, there was a dessert of blueberry cake topped with specially prepared hickory nut ice cream and flakes of chocolate.

Coffee or tea accompanied Martin's remarks.

Martin stood, sipping from his water glass, seemingly as a last moment for remembering before he began to speak. "This has been an amazing journey. In my former life, I thought being president of Supreme Foods was what my life was about. I didn't understand what that meant. The assignment was given to Leland. I was devastated. I also wasn't present when our son went off to service, nor was I present to my wife when our son was killed on a weekend pass. Gladys and I were divorced. My whole life seemed to have no purpose. I tried to hide from life. I took a terrible one room apartment in a part of the city where I felt no one would find me. The room was so terrible I even had to escape from it. I left the room to go to the park across the street. Often I just sat there, not hearing the birds sing, the children at play or any of the rich experiences in the park.

"Also coming to the park was a woman who was to change my life."

Reaching in his pocket, he felt the box with the engagement ring. "Oh, excuse me, I thought this Love Fest was a little dinner this evening. Now you may be our witness." Kneeling down at Beatrice's side, he reached out, taking her left hand and placing the ring on her finger, and shared, "You have taught me to love and awakened me to life. I want to be with you for the rest of our lives. Will you be my wife?" It wasn't what he had practiced but seemed so right at the moment.

Everyone in the room rose up in applause. Some retrieved their handkerchiefs to dry the tears of joy from their eyes. They were thinking, "This is truly a love feast. Would there ever be another Valentine's Day like this?"

Words were not necessary as Beatrice reached over to Martin, still kneeling, and embraced him.

Martin stood, looking lovingly at Beatrice, and then began, "Beatrice came to the park to experience all the life embodied within it. As she wheeled her way into the park, she would greet me. I resisted any response. She persisted. I gradually nodded then said 'hello' or something akin. Then came the day when a terrible storm was looming. There were only the two of us in the park. It began to sprinkle. She began moving as quickly as possible to avoid the rain. She came to me and said, 'Would you help me to my office?' It was my first invitation to life. I jumped up, grabbing the handles of her wheelchair as we raced as fast as we could to avoid getting wet. We laughed, feeling like couple of kids playing a racing game. We got into the church, where her office is, when the cloudburst came, keeping me in the church. She then invited me to push her on to her office. This she had done many times, but it was another invitation.

"Getting inside her office, I moved her behind her desk. I sat looking at her books behind her. There were many books on psychology. Then I looked at her braces. 'You're wondering why I have braces?' I nodded yes. 'When I was seven I contacted polio. I almost died, but I was loved back to life. That is perhaps why my mission is to love others back to life. I have crutches, but I'm more than my crutches!' I replied, "Roberto Assagioli!"

"She replied, 'How do you know Roberto Asesogioli?'" And I said, 'I took a course at The Ohio State University in psychology in preparation of my marketing career. I haven't thought of him since'. She said, 'Then we must talk more.'"

"I looked out the window and saw the rain had stopped. I said, 'The rain has stopped. I must be going. I've spent more time with you in church than I've spent in church the rest of my life.' I left but was feeling something was changing in my life.

"My one room apartment had not changed, but my purpose in going to the park had changed. I looked every day for a time when I would see her. Then came the day when she invited to a breakfast for the homeless at her church. I found many excuses why I shouldn't go. They were all about a fear of being known. But something within me gave in and I went.

"It was there I saw Mr. James. In panic I tried to hide. Mr. James came rushing over, turned me around and greeted me with a warm handshake. Then he invited me to come back to work at Supreme Foods. He expressed more faith and trust in me that I had in myself. That was a powerful affirmation in me and perhaps why I am here.

"I was seated with the homeless people invited to the breakfast. Beside me sat one who was to become a very valued friend. His clothes were tattered, and he was very much in need of a bath."

Ray stood and continued the story. "It was I. My name is Ray Wynn. He invited me to his apartment to try on clothes that he said he planned to give away, and he invited me to shower and shave. Then he took me to his 'little hole in the wall' restaurant for dinner.

After dinner, he wanted to drive me to where I lived. Hesitatingly, I confessed I lived on the street. He said, 'There is room in my apartment for a roll-away-bed. You will be my guest.' With little more food than a box of cornflakes and some milk, I joined him in what seemed to me to be a palace. On a second trip to that same restaurant, he took along a blank tablet and a pen. Dotty, soon to be my wife, was serving us while I drew a picture of Martin. She became very excited about the drawing and called everyone to observe it. From that moment, others in the restaurant wanted me to draw a picture of them. Ultimately, through him, I'm very involved to the work of Supreme Foods.

"By the way, I do have a gift to present of Martin and Beatrice. One morning as we gathered for breakfast, I saw something new in both of them. It was as if their very souls were exposed. I took a picture of them as they waited for their breakfast. This is a painting that I did, revealing a quality of the two of them that I had not seen before in our times together." He unwrapped the package, showing it to Martin and Beatrice, then to the others.

One of the men from the Shipping Department spoke, "Look at the tenderness shown by the way he reaches out to take her hand. And the facial expression as they looked at each other is almost impossible to put into words."

The young man continued, "We are all here because in some small way you've given us so much, that is, our belief in ourselves. For that we are most grateful. Thank you."

"Dr. Bonner did that very thing for me. She invited me to be all I can be. She was always present when I needed to own my condition and be willing to make a change. In the earlier time I thought having a position of power was what I most wanted. What I have discovered is the joy of life is not about having, but how we care about each other and affirm their abilities and their gifts. To that end, I accept the invitation to the presidency of our company. I will do my very best to serve each of you in your journey. Now may I introduce the person who invited me to find my own life: Dr. Beatrice Bonner, who prefers to be called just Beatrice?"

The people stood and applauded long and loudly.

When they returned to their seats, Beatrice said in her strong minister voice, "Thank you for being a part of this Love Fest. There is real power in love. You have shared your love. My birthday is March third. That date will celebrate my birthday and the birth of our two lives together. Our marriage will take place at four P.M. at my church at the edge of the park. Please come and share in another Love Feast."

CPSIA information can be obtained
at www.ICGtesting.com
Printed in the USA
FSOW01n1204061214
3719FS